ETTA
INVINCIBLE

ETTA
INVINCIBLE

BY REESE ESCHMANN

ILLUSTRATIONS BY
GRETEL LUSKY

ALADDIN
New York   London   Toronto   Sydney   New Delhi

ALADDIN

An imprint of Simon & Schuster Children's Publishing Division
1230 Avenue of the Americas, New York, New York 10020
First Aladdin hardcover edition July 2022
Text copyright © 2022 by Charisse Eschmann
Illustrations copyright © 2022 by Gretel Lusky
For information about special discounts for bulk purchases, please contact Simon & Schuster Special Sales at 1-866-506-1949 or business@simonandschuster.com.
The Simon & Schuster Speakers Bureau can bring authors to your live event. For more information or to book an event contact the Simon & Schuster Speakers Bureau at 1-866-248-3049 or visit our website at www.simonspeakers.com.
Book designed by Laura Lyn DiSiena
The illustrations for this book were rendered digitally.
The text of this book was set in Berling Nova.
Manufactured in the United States of America 0622 FFG
2 4 6 8 10 9 7 5 3 1
Library of Congress Control Number 2021937646
ISBN 9781534468375 (hc)
ISBN 9781534468399 (ebook)

For Danny, my love and my best friend,
who is pretty cool

And for my big bro, Rob,
who makes footsteps worth following

ETTA
INVINCIBLE

CHAPTER 1

REALLY WEIRD
WEATHER

PANIC IN
THE CITY AND
THE DISCO

INVINCIBLE GIRL SAVES
THE DAY (AGAIN)

INVINCIBLE GIRL IS THE HERO OF ALL THE STORIES I WRITE.

SHE MOVES BETWEEN BRIGHT WORLDS...

FIGHTING SCALY CREATURES...

AND SUPERVILLAINS

NOTHING CAN STOP HER.

INVINCIBLE GIRL EATS KRYPTONITE FOR BREAKFAST.

SHE'S SO STRONG, SHE MAKES ALL THE OTHER SUPERHEROES JEALOUS.

SERIOUSLY? NONE OF Y'ALL COULD HANDLE THE WEATHER?

GUESS I'LL HAVE TO DO IT MYSELF.

CHAPTER 2

MOM SITS beside me on our front steps, her shoulder rubbing against mine, a swirl of steam from her coffee rising to meet the storm brewing overhead. The sky stretching out above us is a big sheet of gray with clouds like crumpled corners of a page. A few lights flicker on in the windows of the houses and apartment buildings lining our street. Most people are still asking their alarms to let them snooze a little bit longer. Soon they'll be slurping down cereal and fighting over who gets the shower next. But Mom and I are early risers.

There's a question in her eyes. She signs, "Quiet Day?"

I nod.

Mom's big orange hoop earrings sway with the wind. I look at one of the plastic hoops and imagine it hovering in the sky like the sun on a clear summer morning. I'd like to take that sun, stamp it into my sketchbook, and color it in with magic. The hero of the stories I write—*Invincible Girl*—would definitely want to investigate a hoop-earring sun.

That'd be way better than this gloomy gray Thursday situation we've got going on.

"What are you thinking about?" Mom signs.

She only knows the signs for that sentence because she says it all the time—*What are you thinking?* Mom says I'm like a closed book. It's true, because I'm quiet, and also because I put away my sketchbook every time I catch her peeking over my shoulder. Like now.

I snap the book shut. "I'm thinking about Invincible Girl," I say. "But the story isn't ready yet." Mom throws up her arms like she's giving up, but her smile says something else.

On my Loud Days, she has a velvety warm voice that makes my fingers tingle when she sings. She has this Mom-way of making up names for me that don't really make sense, like sometimes I'm Etta (which is normal), but other times I'm this one syllable sung over and over again. On Mondays she sings it slow, like a sigh: *Tahh, Tahh.* On Fridays she sings it fast, like a magic trick: *Ta Da!*

But today is Quiet, and on Quiet Days, Mom's dark eyes reflect all the warmth from her voice. I can't help but return her smile.

"Okay?" she signs.

I nod. I think I mean it.

I have Loud Days, when every car horn is a concert, and Quiet Days, when my own footsteps sound as soft as a ninja mouse. Quiet Days usually come in the spring and summer, when my allergies kick me in the gut and I'm all sneezes and tissues and, *Uh, say that again?*

Quiet is the best way to get lost in heroes and stories. It's like I'm wearing built-in Beats headphones to cancel out all the noises I don't need.

No one ever believes I like Quiet Days. Even my teachers just look at me like I'm a sad little sidekick. Then they talk to me really slowly, as though parting their lips wide when they say *Hello* and pushing their tongues way out of their mouths when they say *Etta* would suddenly make everything Loud again. It doesn't. It just makes them look ridiculous, which I guess would cheer me up if I were sad. (I'm not.)

Or at least I wasn't. My Quiet Days are different now. They're coming more often and there are other, weirder things happening inside my ears—like this ringing sound that's with me now. It's like a high-pitched bird decided an eardrum full of wax was a good place to nest. I wish that bird paid attention to me when I said there were other, better places to lay eggs. Trees, for example. And gutters.

This is my first Quiet Day since I found out about the Big Maybe a few months ago. It's supposed to explain the weirder things and it's kind of a diagnosis, but I call it a Maybe because even my doctors don't know for sure. Dad says it can take time to get answers, and that it's especially hard for Black families because doctors don't always listen to us. That's why Mom went into moving-mountains mode. She signed all three of us up for sign language classes and she's going to have me see another specialist soon. And I love her for that. I *love-love* her for that.

Still, it doesn't change the fact that no one knows what's going on inside me. They don't even know what's going on inside my sketchbook. I wish I could skip to The End of my story, where the hero defeats the villain and the doctors shout, "We figured it out!"

But I'm stuck in the middle. In the Maybe. And not knowing what comes next is as scary as empty panels on a page with no story to fill them.

Writing about Invincible Girl usually fills in all the blanks and the *not knowing* with POWs and SMACKs and comic-colored bravery. But it's been so hard to write lately. Two weeks ago some strange storms blew into Chicago, blocking out the sun and making my allergies act up, so Mom took me back to the doctor. He didn't have any new info about the Maybe, but I've been stuck on my story ever since. Every time I try to work, I can't get past the first few pages of the comic I'm working on.

Mom sets her coffee mug on the steps and pulls a little notebook and a key-chain-sized pen out of her back pocket. She scribbles something down, then flips the notebook around to show me.

I'm glad you're writing again.

I clutch my sketchbook to my chest. My arms are like a big

strong gate, protecting everything that's close to my heart.

Mom looks at me expectantly.

"It's just a few pages. They're only about this nasty weather," I say out loud, scrunching up my nose so she knows my story isn't ready for her to read.

A drop of rain lands on my nose. I look up at the sky and wonder if the weather's watching me. Maybe it gets offended by all the people constantly complaining about it. More raindrops fall from the sky onto my face and my hands, and a weird smell of licorice and smoke fills my nostrils. The storms that have been covering the city with clouds and heavy rains also fill the air with this weird stench. I catch a huge sneeze in my elbow, and Mom and I run inside before the weather ruins my pages for good.

On the TV in the living room, the anchorpeople are talking about the weather, of course. I read the captions on the bottom of the screen.

Chicago enters its third week of record-breaking storms. Civilian advisory boards warn of the negative effects of fifteen straight days without sunlight. Researchers from Rabbit Laboratory continue to study residents complaining of odd spells and low-hanging clouds, but—

That can't be right. *Rabbit Laboratory? Odd spells?* They're probably messed-up captions. The TV's always making mistakes. I'm pretty sure there's no place called Rabbit Laboratory in Chicago, and I bet they meant to say *odd smells*. Mom taps my shoulder. I follow her into the kitchen, and we sit at the antique yellow table in the corner opposite the stove. The table has paint that's rubbed off in some spots and chairs that Mom and I re-covered ourselves after we bought them at a garage sale. It's the coziest corner in our house.

"My story's only about the weather," I say again. Mom told me that when the pages of my sketchbook stay blank, it's because I have writer's block. To me, it feels less like a block and more like a wall so tall that I can't see what's on the other side. I can only hope that there's a world of words and stories over there, and that one day I'll find a ladder.

Can I see? Mom writes. I open my mouth, pretending to be shocked that she would even ask. Didn't she see the face I made outside? She knows I'm embarrassed. When I play out Invincible Girl stories in my head, they look so much better than they actually turn out on paper. Mom says that's okay. Apparently every artist goes through a period when they're waiting for their skills to catch up with their imagination. But my imagination is as fast as the Flash, and my skills are like a slug that doesn't know it's slithering in the wrong direction. I'm not sure I'll ever catch up.

Quit worrying, Mom scribbles. *Writing about what's happening around you is a good strategy. I'll try the same thing. How about at the end of the day, I show you a painting about my day and you show me a story about yours?* Mom's notes take forever to write, but at least her words aren't filled with errors like the captions on the TV. She chooses her words carefully because she cares about me, and that makes it easier to wait for her to finish looping her *l*'s and crossing her *t*'s.

Mom's an artist too. She has a studio upstairs that's filled with canvases and globs of paint. Whatever she makes today will be beautiful. It always is. Mom loves to tell me stories about sketching old buildings in New York when she was in art school, or how that one sunset in Hawaii changed the way she painted the sky forever. She's done enough cool things to know how to turn ordinary skies into awesome skies. But my life isn't interesting enough for an Invincible Girl story. I've never done anything heroic.

Mom might have a point, though. I can't be stuck in the middle forever. I need to go on an adventure or get bitten by a fancy bug or something. Then I can make the very best, most magical comic ever—one that I'll be proud to show her. If I can figure this out, then I can figure *anything* out—even the Quiet and the Maybe.

Mom puts her soft brown fingers on my head. She smooths the hairs that are tucked into two big puffs wrapped with beaded bands. When she does my hair on Loud Days, she tugs at my puffs and asks, "Am I hurting you?" and then keeps on tugging anyway, but today her hands are gentle.

Can't believe I almost let you go to school without fixing these kitchens, she writes after she finishes my hair. She brushes them one more time, and a warm feeling spreads from the hairs at the top of my neck all the way down to my toes. Mom's touch makes me feel like the wall between me and my story isn't quite as tall as the Sears Tower. I let out a deep breath and lean against her, soaking up all the love coming from her sunshiny smile.

It's the kind of love that can't be said with three words. This is love that you record with the camera in your mind and write about in journals and stories and happy-ending movies. Sometimes you love someone so much that you have to say it twice because once is not enough, and even if you'd like to show restraint, the words explode out of your mouth like your soul is made of baking soda and your heart is made of vinegar and your feelings are a science fair volcano waiting to erupt.

I'm about to grab Mom's notebook so I can write, *I love you-love you* when she jots down something else.

You sure you want to go to school today?

I read her words three times and frown. I always go to school.

"What?" I ask, plugging my nose because the weird licorice smell from outside found its way into our kitchen. "You just said I should write a story about my day."

I know I did, she writes. *I'm just double-checking that you're okay. You haven't had a Quiet Day since we got the diagnosis.*

This isn't like Mom. She's usually the one telling me I better go to class even when I want to stay home. Maybe-diagnosis or not, there's no reason I shouldn't go to school. Invincible Girl wouldn't stay away from adventures and villains and math class. She'd be brave, even if she were all sneezy.

INVINCIBLE GIRL (WITH TISSUES FLOATING AROUND HER CAPE): INVIN-**ACHOO**-CI-**ACHOO**-BLE GIRL TO THE RESCUUUACHOOOO!!

"I'm good," I say. "I promise."

Mom rolls her eyes. *Just be careful.* She pauses with her pen floating half an inch above the paper. *You never know when you might have a vertigo—*

I grab the paper from Mom before she can finish writing. I don't want to think about vertigo.

"I said I'm *good*."

Mom stares into my eyes until they start to water and I have to look away. I've never won a staring contest, on account of the never-ending flow of tears always hiding right behind my watery allergy-eyes, ready to burst forth for no good reason at all.

I blink quickly. There are big, fat raindrops sliding down the kitchen window.

"What am I going to do, stay home every time it's Quiet?" I ask. "I love going to school on Quiet Days."

Mom places her right hand on my forehead. I feel a headache coming on, pulsing with a THWACK that feels like a supervillain from my Invincible Girl comics is drilling into my brain.

VERY VILLAINOUS VILLAIN (SNARLING AS HE REVS UP HIS GIANT DRILL): MARK YOUR CALENDAR. IT'S GOING TO BE A LOVELY QUIET DAY ON THURSDAY, BUT ALSO IT WILL SORT OF SUCK, BECAUSE *HAHAHA IT FEELS LIKE I'M DRILLING A HOLE IN YOUR EAR, DOESN'T IT?*

My headaches come with the Quiet sometimes, which doesn't seem fair. It's like when you finally get to eat at a place with burgers and they give you a side salad instead of fries. I've been taking my medicine every day since pollen season came whooshing back like a mean, green hurricane of swirling grass a few days ago, but I knew I'd have a Quiet Day sooner or later. I can feel them coming—it's like a bunch of little beavers live in my ears and they put up a wall to protect themselves from the River of Allergies, but spring comes rushing in and pushes against the wall until so much pressure builds that it bursts.

Mom takes her hand away, but her own forehead is creased with worry.

"Are you sure *you're* okay?" I ask her.

She looks at me, surprised, and writes, *I'm all right. You know how this Chicago weather gets in my bones. I guess I should take a page from your book and get on with my day. You better hurry or you'll miss the bus.*

"I promise I'll write an awesome story for you at school," I say.

Invincible Girl wouldn't stay inside and mope around when there's magic and adventure out there, somewhere.

Mom gives me a half smile.

Keep your phone on you, she writes. *Look both ways when you're walking to the bus. Don't eat anything salty.*

I let out a big sigh that I know she can hear. Mom has always been a health nut, which I guess means she is an almond or something. She takes the train to get to work and then an extra bus to get to the kind of store that sells rainbow chard. She reads every food label three times to make sure all the ingredients are "real," whatever that means. Being a health nut means that some foods are enemies and some foods are friends. When I got the maybe-diagnosis, a whole bunch of new food enemies showed up.

First it was salt.

Then came everything else. Bread. Noodles. Everything with gluten. Anything you can order from a restaurant, and all the yummy snacks that come boxed at the store. They're all packed with sodium. They're all somehow linked to the Big Maybe. *Ménière's disease.* I asked Dad who Ménière was, and he said, "An old white dude, probably."

He was right.

Ménière was a doctor who studied hearing loss. People with Ménière's disease have Loud Days and Quiet Days like me, plus the other stuff like headaches and ringing ears. There's no cure, but there are a bunch of triggers. Like allergies and sodium and moving your head too fast. I imagine the Invincible Girl comic script I'd write if salt were a real villain.

A CROWD OF SCREAMING PEOPLE RUN FROM A MONSTER MADE OF WHITE CRYSTALS.

WHAT IS THAT? A MONSTER? *NO!* IT'S SODIUM!

NO, NO, NOT SODIUM!

IT'S EVERYWHERE!

IT'S IN EVERYTHING!

INVINCIBLE GIRL: IT DOESN'T LOOK SO BAD. IN FACT, IT LOOKS QUITE TASTY. I THINK I'LL HAVE A CLOSER LICK—I MEAN, LOOK.

Mom taps me on the shoulder again. She can always tell when I get lost in my own head. Sometimes my thoughts play out like comic books, a series of scripts and pictures, full of action and adventure. Sometimes I'm in the stories in my head. But Invincible Girl is always the hero.

This is serious, Mom writes.

"I know. I'll be safe."

She watches me as I walk to the bus stop. I pass people getting into their cars or running beneath umbrellas to catch the train down the street. There's a truck with workers outside pumping water out of another flooded basement. No one seems to notice me. Their worlds are loud and their brains are filled with the hum-dum-drums of Thursday morning.

My world is not loud. It whispers with sounds that are hushed and hiding, soft as the sun tiptoeing across the sky.

And my brain is ready for a story.

Invincible Girl doesn't second-guess herself. There's no Big Maybe standing in her way. In fact, there's nothing in the multiverse that can stop her.

Maybe today there's nothing that can stop me.

CHAPTER 3

THERE'S SO MUCH rain that I'm surprised the sidewalk doesn't feel squishy beneath my sneakers. It's April, so I guess we need showers for May flowers or whatever, but this rain is strange and smelly, and it leaves behind clouds that float around my ankles. The clouds have a purplish tint the same color as the lavender plant on Mom's shampoo bottle. They're the kind of clouds that would be fun to stomp through—if the chill in the air didn't cut through layers of clothing and get into your bones. I hope Mom is okay. I wish the sun would come out for a few minutes, just for her, but the sky is dark and gloomy.

I double-check that my umbrella is protecting my back-pack from the rain. No one ever seems to notice that I don't carry schoolbooks in my backpack. I only carry *my* books, the good ones—thick books filled with magic spells, thin books about superheroes who talk in capital letters, and my sketch-book, so long that it barely fits into my bag.

The bus appears down the street. The old wheels bounce more than they roll, and one of them tumbles into the curb near me, sending a puddle of rainwater flying. I take a few steps back so I don't get splashed.

I've been terrified of getting on the bus ever since my first day of kindergarten, when I stepped in a big pile of dog you-know-what while running to my stop, and all my new classmates saw. At least today all I have to worry about is our grumpy cigarette-scented bus driver, Mr. Cole.

Mr. Cole is a white man with brown hair. He always wears a Cubs jersey even though he knows we're on the Sox side of town. And he has way too many rules posted all over the bus, like DON'T USE YOUR SEAT AS A TRAMPOLINE and DON'T GET FINGERPRINT SMUDGES ON THE WINDOWS and DON'T BRING

PETS, ESPECIALLY NOT SQUIRRELS. The weirdest thing is that PUT ON YOUR SEAT BELT is nowhere to be found.

I nod hello to him and watch as his lips spell, "Morning." It's really hard to read lips unless you already can guess a little bit of what the other person is going to say. I've been practicing since I started getting Quiet Days a few years ago, way before the maybe-diagnosis, but I still only catch a few words at a time.

My seat's right in the middle of the bus. There's a giant hole patched with duct tape in the back of the leather seat in front of me. I lean my THWACKing head against the cold window and pull out my sketchbook while Mr. Cole waits for a few more kids to get on. My name is written on the inside cover. I love writing my full name—Laureatte—using the special gold pen that I dip in blue ink. Even though I usually go by *Etta*, I think my full name is so cool, with two *e*'s and two *a*'s and an *L* that swoops beneath all the other letters.

I look up to see a boy with light brown skin and dark hair coming down the aisle. He's a new kid, in seventh grade like me, but we're not in the same class. I think his family moved here a few months ago, but I don't know much about him except that one Loud Day when a kid in the library at school said, "That new kid from Colombia draws a better Miles Morales than you, and he told everyone he's actually Spider-Man." I took offense at that.

I wonder what the new kid's doing, getting on the bus at the same time as me. I'm pretty sure he usually gets on at one of the other stops—maybe he doesn't know his way around yet. There's an invisible line that divides our neighborhood in two. Most of the families on my side are Black, and a lot of the families on the other side are Hispanic. The new kid lives on the other side, where a lady in pink sells corn on the cob and creamy Popsicles out of a big white cart after school. Once I bought a Popsicle over there, but all the labels are in Spanish, and I accidentally ordered a coconut-flavored one, thinking it was vanilla.

The boy is wearing the same orange hoodie that I see him wear all the time, but today it looks different. *It's alive.* There's something squirming around beneath the orange fabric, bulging and protruding like an alien about to burst out of its human host's skin. As I watch, the alien forces its nose up out of the sweatshirt. It doesn't look much like an alien, though. The nose is dark and wet and attached to a snout covered in fluffy golden-brown fur.

The new kid brought his dog on the bus! Now, *that's* something Invincible Girl would do. The dog squirms wildly until its whole head pops out of the sweatshirt, turning the boy into some kind of two-headed creature. I smile without meaning to. The boy looks at me and smiles back. *Oh no.* He thought I was smiling at him. I shrink down into my seat, wishing an alien would beam me up out of here. It should have been obvious I was smiling at the dog, not him. We've never said a word to each other.

The boy plops down on the seat beside me. I wonder what his plan is. Mr. Cole doesn't allow pets on the bus, and I'm pretty sure teachers don't want dogs slobbering on pencils during math class. I brace myself for a sneeze—I'm not supposed to be around dogs. But the sneeze doesn't come. Maybe he has one of those hypoallergenic dogs. That would be cool.

I make eye contact with the dog, which is somehow way

easier than making eye contact with its owner. The dog's fur is thick and fluffy, like cotton candy, and its eyes are so kind-looking that I feel a strong urge to confess my love for all dogs, out loud, right now.

But I don't. Instead I lean in to get a better look at the dog's bright pink collar. There's a small piece of gold metal shaped like a sailboat attached. Tiny words are inscribed on the sail: *I'm not afraid of storms, for I'm learning how to sail my ship. —Louisa May Alcott*

The letters are delicate. They squish together to fit the sail perfectly. I've seen that name—Louisa May Alcott—a million times on the cover of my copy of *Little Women,* a book my dad bought me forever ago when he said I was getting too tall, and he wanted me to stay little. But I've never actually read it—I always end up with She-Hulk or Shuri instead. The words on the sailboat must be from the book or something.

"Louisa?" I ask the dog. "Is that your name?"

The boy nods and scratches her fluffy head. His eyes watch something outside the bus window. Suddenly his eyebrows shoot up toward his hair and he gestures out the window, his lips moving rapidly. The bus drives through a patch of dense lavender-colored fog. I get a strange, shivery feeling, like Mr. Cole just blasted the air-conditioning.

I open my mouth to speak, but I've no idea what to say or if he'd understand me. He's in ESL, so I don't know if he prefers Spanish or English. Most of the bilingual kids our age know both, but I don't know much about his school in Colombia. I probably wouldn't be able to understand him anyway. I snap my mouth shut and hope he doesn't think I'm weird for not saying anything.

Mr. Cole's heavy foot is on the gas now, and the bus bounces by the train station. The elevated trains take people all the way downtown, where the buildings fit together like Tetris pieces and the people walk so fast that they're always bumping into one another. I lean my head against the window and think about Invincible Girl in the sky. She'd know exactly what to say to the boy beside me about the fog and the storms and the—*whoa.*

A black rocket shoots into the air above the south side of the train station. It explodes into tiny pieces that scuttle across the sky like so many beetles. They crawl over the city in a long glittery line that twists into a loopy *E*.

It hovers in front of the clouds, written in the sky like an invitation. I look around the bus, but none of the other kids are staring out the window. Just me and the new kid and Louisa May Alcott, who's squirming and panting in the boy's arms. I turn back to the *E*.

Maybe it's for me.

E for Etta.

My heart beats fast. Not a *thump-thump* like a normal heart—it's a one-two punch straight to a comic book villain's jaw. THWACK-THWACK.

Of course, the *E* could be for lots of other words: *Excited. Exceptional. Elephants.*

Either way, it's strange.

No, it's a word bigger and mightier than strange.

Magical.

And it wasn't part of a comic panel playing out in my head. It's really here—in *my* world. I've never seen a firework like this, not even that time Mom took me to Navy Pier on the

Fourth of July. They don't sell this sort of thing in Indiana, where people in my neighborhood go to buy cheap sparklers and bottle rockets, since you're not allowed to buy them here.

Unless there's a secret magic warehouse in Indiana. Come to think of it, no one's ever told me there *isn't* a secret magic warehouse in Indiana. It's the sort of thing that happens in books. I know some people might tell me, *C'mon, Etta, you're twelve, surely you don't believe everything that happens in books.* But I do. I'm determined to. The shivery feeling I got when the bus drove through the fog comes back, but this time it's more like all the nerves in my body are standing up in excitement, telling me to get closer to the fireworks. I'm not sure if that's a thing that nerves can do. But I feel like the *E* is calling me.

This is it. My chance for an adventure. There's no better story inspiration than magic in the sky. Mom's going to have to pick her jaw up off the floor when she reads my comic.

The boy nudges my shoulder. He's still staring out the window with his eyes wide, even though everyone else on the bus is acting like there's nothing unusual going on. The boy points wildly as a column of purple clouds rolls into the train station down the street. Then the clouds float up into the sky, so thick that they look like the liquid in Dad's old lava lamp. More dark fireworks explode around the clouds, covering the *E*.

The boy lifts up his backpack and shows me the name inked onto one of the straps in black Sharpie.

Eleazar. His name starts with an *E* too. Maybe the magic isn't summoning me. After all, my full name starts with an *L*. Doubt fills my brain, but the shivery feeling doesn't go away.

There's a purplish glow reflected in Eleazar's dark eyes. They widen again, but this time not with awe. His head snaps around to face the aisle. I didn't even realize that the bus had stopped. Mr. Cole stands over us, arms crossed and nostrils flaring. He's got his phone in one hand and a piece of paper in the other. It's a list of all the kids on this route—and it has our parents' phone numbers. I don't need to read Mr. Cole's lips to know what's happening.

He's kicking Eleazar off the bus.

I watch in horror as Mr. Cole speaks into the phone with so much force that beads of sweat drip down his face. After he hangs up, he turns back to Eleazar and shouts so loud his voice bursts through the River of Allergies. "THE RULES SAY DON'T BRING PETS, ESPECIALLY NOT SQUIRRELS! THIS IS THE SQUIRRELIEST DOG I'VE EVER SEEN!" My head aches from all of it. Invincible Girl wouldn't sit quietly while this happened. I could say something, stick up for the new kid, tell everyone that we shouldn't worry about dogs on buses when there are magic fireworks in the sky.

But I don't. I stay Quiet and don't make eye contact with Eleazar or Louisa May Alcott again. I can almost feel the beginnings of my story fading away. The comic panels in my brain empty, and I'm left with nothing but the smell of wet dog and licorice. Magic has no reason to show up in Chicago on a Thursday morning after hiding in books for all my life. I place a hand over my pounding heart and ask myself if I'm sure (very sure) that what I saw is really there. Mr. Cole and the kids on the bus might have been too busy thinking about homework and rules to notice the fireworks, but Eleazar saw them. I know he did.

Invincible Girl would be flying high above the train station now, investigating the sparks and the smoke to see what's real and what's not. I'm not sure I'm cut out for that. My head THWACKs.

If I can't go on adventures, I'll never be able to write about them.

The wind that blows the budding leaves on the trees lining the street doesn't seem to affect the purple clouds still hovering above the train station. I get another jolt of that weird shivery feeling, pulling me toward the train station and the magical fireworks. But I promised Mom I'd be safe. Maybe that's what I should do, even if it means I won't be able to write my comic. The more I think about it, the more I shrink into my seat. I feel like the piece of duct tape covering up the tear in the seat in front of me. I'm barely keeping it together.

I tug on a string hanging from the seat fabric, making the hole even bigger.

The whole bus waits at the side of the road until Eleazar's mom comes to get him. She wears a black suit and one of those faces that says, *I'm not angry, I'm disappointed.* Louisa May Alcott hides her tail between her legs as she hops inside

Eleazar's mom's car. I keep pulling at the tear in the seat as I watch them drive away.

After the fireworks and the dog hidden inside a sweatshirt, seventh grade feels unbearably boring. My live captionist, Ms. Suzy, comes with me to all my classes. In between reading and math, she reminds me to ask for help when I don't understand stuff—she calls this *advocating* for myself. I'd like to advocate for Eleazar and tell Mr. Cole that dogs should be allowed on the bus.

"On the way to school I sat by this kid I haven't talked to before," I blurt out suddenly. "And I wasn't sure how to talk to him."

Ms. Suzy raises an eyebrow. She types into her iPad, "You could try one of the speech-to-text apps we installed on your phone. It won't be as accurate as I am, but it should help you communicate with your friend."

For the rest of the day, I think about the word *friend*. I know that's not what Eleazar and I are, not yet at least. I look around for him in the hallways, but he never shows up.

When I get home after school, Dad tells me that Mom's

still in her studio, working. Probably on her best painting ever. She's still working when I climb into bed, pull out my sketch-book, and stare at the story I started this morning. I write four sentences about the fireworks at the train station, but I scratch them all out. I don't even know what the fireworks were, or whether Eleazar and Louisa May Alcott got in big trouble. I won't be able to get the story right. In the end, I don't write anything. I'm not Invincible Girl.

I'm petrified.

I pull my covers up to my chin and wish the rain and the headaches would stop. So I didn't climb over my writer's block today. But as I fall asleep, I wonder whether that means I won't climb over it ever. I don't want to see Mom's *I'm disappointed* face. And I don't want her to worry about me either. Maybe tomorrow I'll climb over it. I yawn.

I start to dream of fireworks and purple clouds before I even fall asleep. I feel the itch and tingle of beetles crawling over me, and somewhere, deep down, I know: whatever that magic was, it'll find me again.

Or I'll find it.

CHAPTER 4

IN THE MORNING I tiptoe into Mom's studio to peek at the painting she was going to show me, but her canvases are all blank. The big window that usually lets bright yellow light flood into the room shows only darkness outside. There are big blobs of dried paint on one of her palettes—like she poured the colors out but never actually used them. *That doesn't make any sense.* She was working all night.

Mom appears by my side. I startle a little but don't say anything. She slips me her notebook.

How are you feeling?

"Fine," I say. I gesture to all her blank canvases and raise an eyebrow.

Mom's chest rises and falls in a heavy sigh. *I couldn't get any work done yesterday. I was hoping for a little bit of sun to come through those storms, but it never did. I couldn't focus. I'm sorry, I know I promised.*

I think about the thickest bit of purple clouds, the way they formed that column around the train station then floated up into the sky. No light could get through there. I wish the clouds were soft, like big grapes. Invincible Girl would slice them up so the sun could shine again.

"I didn't get much work done either," I say. "Are you going to try again?"

There's a little light that goes on in Mom's eyes, and her mouth turns upward.

Always, she writes.

I return her smile, but something in her expression doesn't feel right. The little pockets under her eyes are puffier than usual.

My eyes catch on some papers on Mom's desk. A bunch of articles about Ménière's disease. *Oh no.* She spent all her time worrying about me. Sometimes, when everyone in my class is acting up and nobody can focus, my teacher says there must be something in the water. Lately it feels like there's something . . . everywhere. Now Mom has a block to get over too? My jaw sets. She always inspires me. Maybe now she needs my help.

"You have nothing to worry about," I say. "I've got an idea for the perfect story. We can swap when I get home from school."

She doesn't ask what my story will be about, which is lucky, because she wouldn't believe me if I told her.

Dad's waiting for me downstairs in the kitchen. His blond-and-brown curls are pulled back with a scrunchie, and his shirt sleeves are rolled up over his elbows. He dances a little while he does the dishes.

"Aren't you going to work?" I ask.

"Nah." Dad fingerspells, "I'm takingamentalhe—"

"Uh, can you slow down?" I ask, trying to figure out what words all of Dad's letters are forming. "You're taking a what? I can't read fingerspelling that fast."

Dad tries again, giving me enough time to piece his letters into words. "I'm taking a mental health day. Got a lot on my mind."

"O-K," I fingerspell back at him. It's going to be a while before we all know ASL well enough to have a regular conversation, but Dad believes in practice making things perfect. He doesn't know a lot of words yet, so he fingerspells everything. It takes even more time than Mom writing stuff down, but I can tell he's super proud of himself.

I smile, but then the River of Allergies whooshes around inside my head. I grab a tissue for my runny nose.

"You okay, She-Hulk?" asks Dad. I don't like the feeling of blowing my nose, but I do like when Dad calls me that.

I get up and wrap my arms around his middle, which is a lot more Hulk-shaped than mine. He always smells like sawdust and bacon grease, but there's something else in the air too.

Licorice and smoke. Yesterday the news said the people at Rabbit Laboratory haven't figured out what makes the storms smell so strange, but I have an idea—*magic*. Magic that rolls into train stations and fills the sky with clouds and fireworks. I walk over to the front window and strain my neck to see down the block. The street is filled with puddles and low lavender clouds. I can see part of the train station down the street. My heart beats a little faster, but there aren't any more fireworks in the sky.

When I had my first series of Quiet Days, all I wanted was to stay home and think about how unfair it was that I sneezed all the time and couldn't get a cat. I was only in third grade then, and we didn't know anything about Ménière's disease. But we did have a hermit crab named Michael who could tuck his whole body inside a small green seashell. Dad said Michael and I were cut from the same cloth and our house was like my shell. Then he closed the curtains and cut off all the lights before chasing me around the house until we collapsed from laughing.

And then we flicked on the lights, opened the curtains, and went outside to face the villainous grass pollen and enjoy the Quiet. I didn't want to be a hermit crab. I wanted to be brave.

I still do.

I can't stay inside any longer. I have to do this. For me and for Mom.

Something out there is pumping columns of purple clouds into the sky and making fireworks trace *E*s above the city. I'm going to find out what it is and find a way to slice those clouds up so Mom can work again. I already have a tagline for my new comic: *Invincible Girl faces Petra Fide in the ultimate showdown: superstrength vs. super-weird fireworks.*

First I need to find the only other person who saw the magic. Eleazar. He can be the Robin to my Batman, if he wants.

I slide my phone in my pocket, put my sketchbook in my backpack, and tell Dad that I'm going to school, even though it's too early for the bus. He gives me the same *Be careful* talk that I got from Mom yesterday, except he tries to pretend like he's only worried because it's so dark out—and not because of the maybe-diagnosis. I remind him that I've been walking around on my own since I turned twelve last year, then give him an extra hug before I leave.

The street we live on is part of the invisible line that divides our neighborhood. I've never had a friend from the other side. Actually, I've never had a friend on any side of any street, only my cousins, who have a giant trampoline, and my auntie, who lets me sit next to her when she's playing spades with Mom. That's because I was quiet even before I started having Quiet Days. Invincible Girl doesn't have many friends either. She's too busy saving the world and bodybuilding.

I cross the street and walk up and down the unfamiliar blocks, but it's no use. I can't find Eleazar or Louisa May Alcott anywhere. Maybe they live farther away than I thought, or they're still asleep. Eventually I give up and head back. Then I see them—they're on the corner near my house. Louisa walks in front of Eleazar, pulling hard on a long yellow leash.

They're walking in the direction of the train station. Maybe Eleazar felt the same pull that I did yesterday, like the magic was summoning me. I look for fireworks in the sky, but there's nothing. I don't know whether to be relieved or disappointed—so instead I walk faster to catch up with Eleazar. I check the time on my phone. We still have half an hour before the bus comes. I wonder if he's going to go home and drop off Louisa before school. There's no way he's going to try to sneak her onto the bus again.

Eleazar has a stuffed-to-the-brim messenger bag at his side and a big green sketchbook tucked under his elbow. I gasp. It's the same as mine. The only one they sell at Walgreens. I wonder if it's filled with stories too.

As I trot to catch up with them, I think about shouting something to let them know I'm here. I wouldn't mind exploding like a fancy firework, but all my emotions have ever managed are a small crackle and pop. Just then, I see the fireworks rise into the sky again. This time the rocket is green, and it explodes in a burst of dark smoke. Small purple lines emerge from the smoke. They twirl through the air like a person in a big skirt who can't stop spinning. The lines form another *E* in the sky. It could be for *Etta*. Or *Eleazar*.

Or both of us.

Another shiver runs through me. Something—or someone— is definitely calling to us. But why? The sky opens up and speaks in a whirl of rain that splatters over the streets. Eleazar and Louisa May break into a run.

I speed up, going as fast as I can while opening up my umbrella to protect my hair and my books. I follow them down the street until I reach the stairs beneath the train station.

I swipe the Ventra card Mom gave me for emergencies. Eleazar and Louisa already went through. The tips of my fingers tingle, and my hand shakes a little, like the purple clouds are moving around and making a storm inside me. I take deep breaths with every step up to the elevated platform, trying to prepare myself for whatever awaits us. The clouds surrounding the station form a purple rainbow. The ones at the bottom are a light lavender, but they get darker and denser as I go up the stairs. At the very top, the clouds are the deepest violet color. I can barely see the cars on the street below the station.

E for *Enchanted.* That's how the platform feels, at least. The clouds hide the train tracks from the rest of the city.

Eleazar is standing on the platform. He turns as soon as I reach the top.

He smiles like he's not surprised to see me. Then he beckons me over immediately.

I look around, expecting the world to have changed now that magic has filled the sky. There should be people with cameras and little kids jumping up and down and a news reporter asking me what I think the *E* stands for. But Eleazar and I are the only people standing on the platform. The board with the train schedule says there's not supposed to be another arrival for twenty minutes. We're caught in the empty space between the last train and the next train.

But there's magic in the empty space. I can feel it.

A dark shape appears on the tracks, surrounded by rolling purple clouds. My feet feel a little wobbly. It's an early train. An *eerie* train. The shape grows larger.

My mouth falls open.

The train pulling into the station is massive and *impossible* and colored more brilliantly than any comic I've ever seen. The tracks beneath it turn from rusty brown to bright gold as it approaches, and a sparkling purple cloud hovers above the engine. More fireworks escape from the smokestack. They're much smaller than the ones we saw earlier. If the first fireworks were an invitation written in the sky for all to see, this burst is a note passed in class when the teacher isn't looking. It's secret and special. I shiver as I take in the rest of the train.

The front is covered in pipes and rods and chimneys that remind me of trains from old books about traveling west, but nothing else about it looks like any train that's ever existed, now or in old books. The cars are made of sleek black metal glittering with swirling swaths of color. I look behind me, half expecting to see that an odd-colored rainbow is responsible for the reflection, but the sky is empty. When I turn back to the train, the colors fold into one another more like a painting than a reflection, and they grow across the bottom of the train like bright, giant flowers.

The sort of magic that happens in books is right in front of my face—made of steel and color and smoke instead of tiny printed words.

It's real. My heart flutters in my chest. I blink slowly, waiting for the train to vanish each time my eyelids close.

Tears push against the corners of my eyes, but not because I'm sad. I'm awed.

A shiver of wonder moves from the tips of my fingers to the THWACK-THWACK of my heart pounding in my chest. It only takes a moment longer for worry to mix in: Of all the kids who might get the chance to stand in front of a magic train, why me? Why *us*? I watch as thick purple smoke comes out of the smokestack, pumping into the sky, surrounding the train and the station. It looks odd—there's dark, gloopy tar coming out of the smokestack too. Dad would say that engine needs a tune-up for sure. Maybe that's why the train wanted us here. It needs our help. But I don't even know how to change the tires on my bike.

Beside me, Eleazar's eyes are wide and excited. He pushes a big piece of dark hair away from his face and holds his messenger bag steady at his side.

The train is pointed toward downtown, but it doesn't move. Of course a magic train doesn't pull into a stop just to sit there. It's waiting for passengers. And it called *us*.

Louisa May Alcott's tail wags excitedly.

We walk down to the only entrance—a big black door on the very last train car.

It slides open. I take two steps back, almost tripping over my own feet. Eleazar does the opposite—two leaps forward.

A purple carpet rolls out the door, covering the concrete platform with a soft, bright path. Louisa May runs forward and sniffs it, pulling Eleazar behind her. He holds the yellow leash with two hands to keep her from slipping away. Invincible Girl would follow them, but I'm too nervous to move. I don't think Mom would be happy if I missed the bus because I was riding magical trains around town.

This is what I wanted, isn't it? I can't write about adventures without having them myself.

I finally know how to fill the pages of my comic—with magic and fireworks and a train on golden rails.

All I have to do is walk up to that carpet, and I'll see what's on the other side of the wall in my brain. I'll be able to write my story.

I look up to the sky for courage, but the movement of the purple cloud above the train makes me dizzy. My headache pulses back into my temples. I shut my eyes tight. Dizzy spells and ringing in my ears aren't normal for Quiet Days. They're exactly what Mom was worried about yesterday.

The scariest thing about my maybe-diagnosis isn't headaches or Quiet. It's vertigo.

If pain is rude, then vertigo is just plain evil. It takes hold of your body and makes you feel like you can't control any of your limbs. The whole world spins and your stomach flops around until you get sick. It happened to me a few months ago when I was walking to the store to get some candy. It's why I have the maybe-diagnosis and why Mom is so worried about me being out by myself. But I know what to do if it happens—which it isn't.

No, I'm fine, I tell myself. I don't have vertigo right now. The magic smoke twirls fast enough to make anyone dizzy. Maybe even Louisa May.

I focus on the ground instead, avoiding the shifting colors on the side of the train.

There's a spot of stepped-on gum on the platform that's probably been stuck here for ages. *Like me.*

When the world stops spinning, I take small steps up to the purple carpet. My breaths come in sharp little gasps. I look inside the train's open door from a few feet away—my body won't let me get any closer. The only thing I can see in there is a bunch of bluish light.

Eleazar keeps both feet planted on the carpet outside as he inspects the train car. He holds tight to Louisa's yellow leash as her fluffy tail disappears inside the train. I wonder why he's not running on with her. He doesn't look scared—but maybe scared isn't always a look. He might be as nervous as me.

There's a small sign nailed next to the door. It looks like the front of Dad's old digital alarm clock, with glowing red letters instead of numbers.

BOARDING

The carpet beneath Eleazar ripples like a gentle wave. It wants us to come on board too.

THWACK. THWACK. My head aches and my heart beats fast. All my villains are back in full force.

The sign on the train changes.

THINKING ABOUT BOARDING

I lift my right foot, but it feels as heavy as a backpack full of math books. The purple carpet moves again.

It would only be a few more steps to get on.

I can imagine Invincible Girl jumping onto the train. Her cape takes her everywhere, from my world to hers, to face any sort of magic or mischief.

INVINCIBLE GIRL (STRETCHING HER ARMS): GOOD MORNING, MYSTERIOUS TRAIN! TAKE ME TO THE PLACE WHERE ALL THE TROUBLE IS.

The thought of an adventure pulls me forward, but the

ringing in my ears tells me not to move a muscle. Mom was nervous about me going to school. She'd never let me get on a train alone. And my doctor says stress can lead to vertigo. Maybe a blank page is better after all.

The sign changes again.

PROBABLY NOT BOARDING

The train knows I'm not as brave as Invincible Girl—and apparently not even as brave as a goldendoodle.

I look back at the arrivals board. Only two minutes until the next train and—*uh-oh*. We've already missed our bus. I look at the time again. If I leave now, I may never find out why the train called us here. But if I stay and don't make it to school, Mom'll be so upset. I might still be able to catch the bus at the stop right past the train station. "Eleazar," I cry. "We missed the bus—we need to go!"

He looks between me and the train, like he's trying to make up his mind. But then something startles him. He looks up at the sky and his eyes widen. Above us the thick clouds are as dark as night. They swirl together like a tornado, and streaks of violet lightning rip through them. Eleazar tugs on Louisa's leash, but she doesn't come back out. The sign changes again.

ALL ABOARD.

Oh no.

In a smooth, quick motion, the carpet pulls from beneath Eleazar's feet and rolls back into the train. He stumbles backward, and Louisa's leash slips out of his grasp. The door slides shut.

My hand extends automatically, but my feet are still stuck to the ground like gum. Invincible Girl would fly over to help Eleazar, but I don't know how to fly, and I can't get my legs to walk.

The train takes off with Louisa inside and Eleazar outside.

Eleazar reaches for the train, but it slips past him, gaining more and more speed until it's gone. The rails turn gold as the train moves toward the city.

My head spins. This can't be happening.

"Louisa!"

My panicked cry doesn't make the train come back. It doesn't get my feet unstuck, either.

A few seconds pass, and it's like the train was never here. The tracks turn back to rusty reddish brown, and no one would believe a magical train had stopped for us, if it weren't for Eleazar, his missing dog, and the purple clouds that twist above the empty railway.

Eleazar turns toward me. He opens his mouth, about to speak.

Overhead a boom of thunder breaks through the River of Allergies again. *Ouch.*

I look into Eleazar's eyes. They're filled with something deep and dark and sad.

He knows what I know.

Louisa May Alcott isn't on the sort of train that'll drop her off at the next stop in a few minutes.

She's gone.

CHAPTER 5

"I'M SORRY," I call out.

A crowd of people push their way to the platform to catch the next train, filling the space between Eleazar and me. They have no idea what happened here. Before I know it, I've lost Eleazar in the crowd. My phone buzzes. It's a text from Mom.

Your location looks off. Did you catch the bus okay?

Must be the storm messing stuff up, I text back. Then I look around for Eleazar one more time, with no luck. And I run.

I maneuver around people to get down the stairs, and spot a blur of the big yellow bus down the street past the station.

I race after it, waving my hands wildly. My shirt sticks to the back of my neck, my socks soak through in the rain, and a high-pitched ringing makes a home in my brain.

The school bus skids to a halt half a block ahead, and dark purple smoke escapes from the exhaust.

I can feel my classmates' eyes on me as I run for the door, my backpack bouncing awkwardly behind me. My feet slow to a casual stroll when I reach the bus steps. I turn my head away from the cigarette-scented wrath twisting Mr. Cole's face, plop down on my seat like I'm totally normal (because I am), and look out the window like everything's cool (which it definitely isn't).

My heart THWACKs fast, and my ears ring. I look around for Eleazar. *Where did he go?*

I swing my backpack around to the front as I sit down.

It's empty. I never zipped it shut when I left the house this morning. All my books fell out when I was running. My comics and all the stories I've ever written are out there some-where, soaking up the rain and turning into pulp. I stand up to try to get off the bus, but it lurches forward and slams me back into my seat. *No.* My teachers say that writing is the only way to make something live forever, but if they're right, then why do words always seem so fragile? Paper burns, ink fades, and careless kids like me drop their books in puddles.

I close my eyes. If I can't hear Mr. Cole scolding me for missing my stop and being very wet, he probably isn't. And if he is, the other kids must think I'm very, very cool to be ignoring it so well. I didn't want this to be the reason why I became cool on a Quiet Day. I wanted to find magic for my story, but instead I ran. Now the rest of my comics and all my sketches about Invincible Girl are lost and ruined. And Louisa May is gone. A big guilty ache takes over the place where my heart should be.

I'm thinking about how to escape the bus to go back to the train station when I see a blur of orange speeding down the street. Eleazar has *two* green sketchbooks tucked under his arm—along with a few thin comic books and his messenger bag. He stopped to pick up my books.

But he's getting left behind.

The bus lurches forward again.

✦

I press my cheek against the window so I can see him. My throbbing temple pulses against the cold glass. Eleazar looks up, right at me, and I slam my palm against the window as we roll away.

Cigarette smoke mixes with the charcoal and licorice. Mr. Cole speeds up. I raise my hand to tell him that there's another student waiting, but he glares at me in the rearview mirror and points to one of his rule signs. NO HAND RAISING. Purple sparks escape the end of a cigarette I don't think he's supposed to have. He tosses it out the window and coughs without covering his mouth. Mr. Cole's breath leaves a gray-violet smudge on the windshield. Maybe the storm got into his lungs the way it got into Mom's bones.

I put my hand down and fall back into my seat, eyes fixed on Eleazar as he runs behind the bus.

He's *fast*—to me, he seems faster than those spandex-covered sprinters in the Olympics. He can't really be Spider-Man, of course, but with the rain and the purple clouds surrounding him, he looks like a hero ripped right from the pages of a comic book.

Our bus picks up more speed. We roll through a stop sign as we turn left, and start flying down the straight, eight-block street that leads to the school—I am definitely going to call the How Am I Driving number on the back of the bus as soon as I escape this thing.

Eleazar's feet start moving faster than our wheels, and I think he's probably going to pass the speed of sound or tear a hole in the universe.

A mean-looking crossing guard standing under an umbrella holds up a stop sign right before Eleazar can cross the block behind us. He stops and breathes heavily before bending his knees, ready to explode. As soon as the crossing guard turns his sign, Eleazar takes off again, running past purple-tinted streetlights. Faster than ever.

We've only got three blocks before we get to school. Eleazar catches up when the bus gets stuck behind a delivery truck. He isn't just going to make it; he's going to *beat us*. I open my window and start to whoop in what I think must be a very loud voice, because other kids rush to see what I'm seeing. Mr. Cole can't say anything because he's got no rules about seat belts.

The other kids watch in awe as Eleazar catches up, then passes the bus, his orange hoodie still flapping around in the wind.

Now everyone is cheering and no one cares that the bus is tilting to the left, because we're only one block from school. Mr. Cole shakes his fist at Eleazar and pushes harder on the gas, but the old yellow bus is too slow. Eleazar reaches the circle in front of our school building before we do, and I sit back in my seat, holding my hand over the THWACKs that move down from my head to my chest. The cheers of the other kids are muted in my ears, but I can feel the energy in our pile of jumbled-up kids. When we pull up in front of the school, I push past everyone to get down the steps so I can talk to Eleazar before the other kids surround him.

Up close he doesn't look superhuman. I don't think he got any weird powers from the train. He's just superfast. A big chunk of dripping-wet hair is stuck to his forehead, and his fingers dig into the side of his stomach as he tries to catch his breath. His clothes are covered in specks of rain. Other kids walk by and point at him or give him high fives, but he just shrugs and waves them inside. We escape the rain beneath a small awning at the main door of the school. I sit on a small spot of dry pavement with my back against the brick wall. Eleazar joins me.

He hands me my small pile of books, holding on to his own sketchbook. My fingertips close around the damp pages, and I let out a huge breath. Some of the ink on the cover of my comics got smudged, and everything is a little soggy, but it's in pretty good shape.

"I'm so sorry about Louisa," I say. There are still thick purple clouds down by the train station, and the rest of the sky seems even darker than before. I think I can feel the storms seeping into my bones, just like Mom. I wrap my arms around my middle and wish that Louisa were here so I could pet her fluffy, warm fur.

Eleazar's lips move, but I don't catch his response. Sounds get stuck in my ears on Quiet Days, like the sounds trapped inside a giant seashell. It's more intense when there are lots of noises around. Individual voices are the hardest to pick out, because words are so delicate and everyone says them at a different pace and in a different tone.

"What?" I say. "Sorry, um, I'm hard of hearing. I can lip-read a little, but I don't know Spanish. I've been learning how to use my phone, if you want to try . . ."

My words trail off at the end. It's weird to talk out loud on Quiet Days when the sound pushes back against all the extra fullness of the river in my ears.

I take out my phone and open Google Translate, like Ms. Suzy suggested. Mom and Dad are old-school and always want to write or practice signing, but maybe Eleazar will like this. He looks over my shoulder as I set the app to conversation mode.

"So the phone is pretty bad at punctuation and stuff. And it messes up some words. But, uh, do you want to use English or Spanish?"

Eleazar shrugs. "I speak both."

He watches his words appear on my screen. Eleazar hesitates, then taps a button so Google Translate will listen for Spanish, too.

"Cool," I say. He speaks both, but maybe one language is more comfortable than the other. I think I understand that.

The words "Cómo te llamas?" appear on my screen as Eleazar speaks, with the English translation underneath. "What's your name?"

Before I can respond, Eleazar takes the phone and keeps talking into it. The translation reads, "Can you understand me when I'm talking fast? Can you understand me when I'm talking slowly?" He pauses, then gives a satisfied nod. "Bacano."

The last word doesn't translate. He deletes it and repeats himself in English. "Cool." He passes the phone back to me.

"My name is Etta. And I'm sorry about Louisa," I say again, watching as my words translate and the app says out loud, "Mi nombre es Erica. Y lo siento por Louisa." I change *Erica* to *Etta* and repeat myself one more time for good measure. I read the translation of Eleazar's words as he responds.

"It's okay," he says. "We rescued her, and her previous owners told us she blows up a lot but always go back."

"Huh?" I ask. That doesn't sound right. I think Google Translate got something confused. Even though the phone is helping, I wish Ms. Suzy were here. She'd know what he meant. "She blows up a lot?"

Eleazar frowns at my phone. I hand it to him, and he types, "Run."

"Oh," I say. "She runs . . . runs away a lot? So—you're not worried?"

Eleazar shrugs and shakes some rainwater out of his hair.

"I'm going to get her after school."

If I were him, I wouldn't just be worried. I would be made of worry, from head to toe, every cell in my body freaking out. But he's so calm. He seems more and more like a superhero. Then I notice his left leg, and the way it bounces up and down on the pavement, and I notice that his fingernails are digging into his palms. He *is* worried. I wonder why he doesn't say so.

The front door opens and our gym teacher comes out. My phone picks up her words but misses some of the punctuation. "What are y'all doing out here? Your class went through that door, and Eleazar, I thought you were in the gym."

She pulls Eleazar in through the front door. Neither of them look back at me.

I didn't even get to thank him for saving my books, but it's okay.

There's a new story forming inside my head.

CHAPTER
6

I SPEND MY WHOLE art block designing a thank-you comic for Eleazar. But it's more than that. It's a thank-you and a promise.

After school I'm going to help him get Louisa May Alcott back.

As soon as Ms. Suzy goes on break during art class, I slide my phone out of my pocket. I'm allowed to use it in school on Quiet Days, but she also says I am *not* allowed to use it for all the normal seventh-grade things like texting and flirting and taking "bored at school" selfies. Not that I'd want to send a selfie to anyone.

And this card counts as art anyway; it's not the sort of thank-you that you mumble to overzealous line leaders who hold the door or to moms who plop mushy spaghetti onto your plate. (My mom just started making spaghetti out of *squash*, and I am not okay.)

We have art class in a spare room in our school's basement. I'm sitting in the back corner, away from the other kids. The white light stuck in the ceiling is almost too bright compared to the storms outside. I stare at the pages of my sketchbook and imagine them as a wet, mushy pile of pulp. Mom would have taken me to Walgreens to buy another one from the stack of green-covered books, but it wouldn't have been the same. It wouldn't have been *mine*. All my work on Invincible Girl would have disappeared, and my stories would have washed away in the rain just like voices get washed away in the River of Allergies.

So my card has to show the sort of gratitude that tugs and pulls at the strings around your heart, so much that it almost hurts, and instead of saying something, you just produce hundreds of sparkly, salty tears. The first time I felt this sort of oh-thank-you-so-much-you-have-no-idea-how-badly-I-wish-I-weren't-crying gratitude, I was five. I'd gone to my first birthday party that had real cake—not shredded zucchini squares, sweetened with agave, but *real* cake—vanilla dotted with melted Funfetti sprinkles and slathered with goopy milk chocolate frosting. I'd never had cake like that, and I knew my mom would never let me try a piece (I mean, she was already annoyed that the party hats barely fit over my hair), but then she picked up the plate with the biggest slice and set it right in front of me. I burst into tears before the sweetness even touched my lips. They were the same sort of tears that pushed against my eyes at the train station. Not sad. Not really happy, either. Just awed.

But my thank-you comic can't be all tears and awe and cake. It needs a villain. Every good story has one. I get to work on the script.

DR. PETRA FIDE STANDS AT THE FRONT OF A SPEEDING TRAIN CAR, HER BULKY LASER GUN AT HER SIDE. THE SHARP, POINTED HEEL OF HER SHOE RESTS ON A PILE OF BOOKS.

DR. PETRA FIDE: AS SOON AS I DESTROY THESE MANUSCRIPTS, I'LL BE UNSTOPPABLE! NO ONE WILL BE ABLE TO PROVE I WAS BEHIND THE STORMS.

INVINCIBLE GIRL PUNCHES HER WAY THROUGH THE DOOR AND INTO THE TRAIN CAR.

INVINCIBLE GIRL: GO AHEAD AND TRY.

DR. PETRA FIDE: YOU THINK YOU CAN DEFEAT ME ALL BY YOURSELF?

INVINCIBLE GIRL: OH, DEFINITELY NOT.

A CLOSE-UP PANEL OF PETRA FIDE'S CONFUSED FACE.

INVINCIBLE GIRL: I DON'T HAVE TO. I'M NOT ALONE.

THE DOOR TO THE TRAIN CAR BEHIND PETRA FIDE OPENS. A CURLY-HAIRED DOG RUNS THROUGH AND KNOCKS FIDE OVER. A BOY WEARING AN ORANGE CAPE APPEARS BEHIND HER, GRABS THE PILE OF BOOKS, AND RUNS AWAY SO FAST THAT HE BECOMES AN ORANGE BLUR.

DR. PETRA FIDE: INVINCIBLE GIRL, THIS IS NOT THE END! I'LL GET YOU, AND YOUR LITTLE DOG TOO— AAAAAAAHH!

PETRA FIDE YELLS AS INVINCIBLE GIRL'S FOOT STEPS OVER HER FACE.

INVINCIBLE GIRL: WHOOPS, SORRY ABOUT THAT, PETRA. YOU KNOW ME. SO CLUMSY. CATCH YOU LATER!

I can't help myself from smiling as I fill in the drawings.
My story's finally taking shape.

Beneath the comic I write a note for Eleazar. I use Google
to translate the comic and the note.

> *Dear Eleazar,—Estimado Eleazar,*
>
> *Thank you for saving my books.—Gracias por*
> *salvar mis libros.*
>
> *We don't know each other very well, but I think*
> *you're a hero (and I know a lot about heroes).—*
> *No nos conocemos muy bien, pero creo que eres un*
> *héroe (y sé mucho sobre héroes).*
>
> *I promise I'm going to help you get Louisa back.—*
> *Prometo que te ayudaré a recuperar a Louisa.*
>
> *After that, maybe we can be friends.—Después de*
> *eso, tal vez podamos ser amigos.*

I smile again.

My story didn't end with PROBABLY NOT BOARDING.
It starts like this.

I reread the thank-you promise. The letters in the last sentence are extra lovely and bold, but I can't stop thinking about

the word *friend*. Maybe that's what I needed for my Invincible Girl story all along—a spark of magic and a partner. A different kind of THWACK pounds in my chest—an almost hopeful one, but it feels heavy, too. *Eleazar might not want to be my friend.*

He's probably not thinking about friendship when Louisa's missing. I remember her sweet eyes and how I wanted to tell her I loved her right away. She's the reason why I have to help even if Eleazar and I aren't quite friends yet.

After school I text Mom that I'll be a little late. I find Eleazar outside, and we sit in the same spot where we talked earlier, while the rest of the kids chase each other around the concrete lot. I pull the thank-you comic out of my sketchbook and extend the pages cautiously. It's been a long time since I showed anyone else my comics.

As soon as the pages are in Eleazar's hands, a million worries fill my brain. My drawings look like a preschooler made them. My story is silly. I should never, ever let anyone read my work. Eleazar looks at the comic for seconds that feel like hours—*he probably hates it*—before he pulls out his own sketchbook and hands it to me.

He's cool with me looking at the whole thing? He doesn't apologize for the quality or ask me to skip pages 5 to 10 or anything.

I open the sketchbook and gasp. It's filled with the most beautiful drawings I've ever seen. A swirl of pastel smudges makes a purple cloud in the sky. There are sketches of Spider-Man and Black Panther and about a hundred drawings of Louisa. He's drawn speech bubbles everywhere, and they're filled with words like POW! And KABANG! He has this cool-looking way of shading in the speech bubbles with thin, super-straight lines, and all the colors are bright and bold. On the last page there's an outline of a girl and a dog standing in front of a train. *It's me.*

"Whoa," I breathe. I open Google Translate on my phone as Eleazar stares at my comic.

"Bacano," he says.

It's the same word that didn't translate before. It meant *cool.* And he does look like he likes the comic. I smile bigger than I mean to. "Let's walk to the train station together."

"You really want to help?" he asks.

"I promised I would."

I almost want to take my promise back and run home,

but my feet are stuck to the ground again, like they were this morning when I saw the train. At least this time it's for a better reason. *Because I made a promise, and you can't take those back.*

He waits for a second, watching me closely, like he thinks I'm going to take off too. But I don't. We walk together down the street. Luckily, it's not raining as much as it was earlier. And I triple-checked that my backpack was zipped, anyway.

There are hardly any purple clouds at the train station when we get there. It looks so *ordinary*. People swipe their Ventra cards and look at their phones while they're waiting for the trains. Eleazar and I look all over for Louisa, but she's definitely not at the station. He texts his mom to see if Louisa already made it home . . . but no luck. My heart sinks. If I'm not home soon, Mom will start to wonder what happened to me. But there's no sign of the magic train. Maybe I was seeing things because I wanted to find magic so badly. But Louisa really disappeared. Magic or not, some kind of train took her—but would it come back?

Eleazar looks frustrated. I read his translated words. "Do you think the storms are coming from the train?"

I think for a second. "I—I don't know," I say. "But the clouds were thickest here, don't you think? They were coming from the smokestack and filling the sky."

He nods. "And there was thunder after the gunpowder."

I read his words on my phone. "Gunpowder?"

Eleazar shakes his head. "I don't know the right word."

He reaches inside his messenger bag, grabs his sketchbook and a pen, and balances the book on his arm. He draws the letter E with a bunch of lines and stars extending from it.

"The fireworks! I didn't notice the thunder," I say. "If the train is the reason for the storms and the clouds blocking out the sun, then maybe we can stop it. When we find the train, we can figure out how to turn the engine off or something. It might need a tune-up, you know, like an oil change."

Eleazar looks doubtful. My voice falters. I have no idea how to stop the storms. I think about the gloopy tar coming out of the smokestack, and shudder. The purple carpet and the E in the sky were so inviting, but the storms and the tar are less friendly. I don't know what—or who—we'll find when we get on the train. Mr. Cole and the other kids didn't notice the fireworks. And the news never said anything about storms coming from the train station. But Eleazar and I can't be the only ones who were called to it—right? "Do you think we should tell someone?" I ask. "Maybe they could help us."

He speaks into my phone. "Who should we tell? The police?"

I frown. "What are the police gonna do with a magic train? Shoot it?"

In the end we decide to tell the CTA worker who's there to help with broken train cards and stuff. When I ask her to speak clearly into my phone, she decides we're pranking her and tells us to go home.

"There's a new curfew starting tonight anyway," she says.

"Curfew?"

"Citywide. People are getting uneasy about these storms. Over two weeks with no sun isn't good for anybody." She shakes her head. "Y'all better get home."

"Louisa May Alcott is my best friend. I can't lose her."

Eleazar looks uneasily around the station like he's still hoping she'll show up. He uses his left hand to squeeze all the fingers on his right hand, but when he sees me watching, he stops and balls his fingers into fists.

"I'm going to stay here," he says.

"But what about the curfew?"

"I don't care."

I stare at the words on the translator. I don't know what it's like to lose a best friend, but I know what it's like not to have one. I try to come up with something that'll make him feel better.

"The fireworks were here yesterday and today. And we know they come from the train." The realization hits me as I say it. "Actually, we saw the fireworks at the same time both days! That must mean the train is on a schedule! We can get on and find Louisa tomorrow."

I hope my voice sounds confident and brave and not like someone who doesn't know a thing about magic train schedules.

"I can't wait until tomorrow," protests Eleazar.

"It's only a few more hours. And tomorrow's Saturday, so we'll have all day." I wonder what Mom will think of the new curfew, but I push that thought away.

"I shouldn't have let go of her. Louisa always flies. Now I'm here all alone."

He pushes his fists together. *I try to make sense of Eleazar's* words. *My brain hurts. I'm tired of having to figure out my phone's mess-ups. But Eleazar looks tired too. He probably didn't mean that Louisa flies like an airplane or a superhero. But she did fly away from us, in a way. And it seems like he thinks it's his fault she's missing.*

My phone buzzes. It's Mom telling me I better be home for dinner soon.

"You couldn't have known the train was going to leave. We'll find Louisa together. Come to my house, and we'll make a plan."

Eleazar opens his mouth, but I keep talking.

"She'll be there tomorrow," I say. "And if she's not, w-we'll search every block in the whole city until we find her!"

At least that's what Invincible Girl would do.

"Seriously?" asks Eleazar.

My brain screams no.

"Yeah," I say. And then I use the word again—the big one that I can't take back. "I promise."

CHAPTER 7

ELEAZAR AND I walk home together from the train station. The streetlights are on early. Their yellow-tinted glow makes the clouds dancing over the ground look extra creepy. In the houses we pass I see people who know nothing about the train, going about their business, leaning back on reclining chairs and watching TV. I wonder whether they can feel the storm in their bones too, but I mostly pay attention to the ringing in my ears. About a minute later I notice that Eleazar's lips are moving. *Whoops.*

The ringing in my head gets louder, like a barrier between

my ears and the world. It reminds me of the barrier between me and Eleazar. My phone helps, but it's not the same as having Ms. Suzy around, telling me exactly what people are saying. The odds are stacked against us, like the potential for our friendship is measured by a test you have to take with no calculator and no pencils. Mom says a lot of things are stacked that way.

I pull out my phone even though a few drops of rainwater fall onto the screen.

"I hate the rain here," he's saying. "In Colombia when it rained, it was still good weather and heat. Even the snow would be better than jumping through frozen puddles."

I raise an eyebrow. Eleazar lived through February in Chicago. He should know better than to wish for dirty piles of slush over a little bit of rain. But I don't blame him for not feeling excited about magical storms.

"Louisa doesn't like the rain either," he adds.

I think about the words on Louisa May Alcott's dog tag. *I'm not afraid of storms, for I'm learning how to sail my ship.* I hope she's not afraid. I wish she were here with us. I'd pet her and tell her that wet-dog smell doesn't bother me at all.

"It's okay," I say, hoping that my voice doesn't come out as shaky as it feels. "She's on the train. I bet she's nice and dry. We'll get her back tomorrow."

"I know." Eleazar's words appear on my screen, but there's no way to tell whether there was any doubt in his voice. I don't know if I believe my own words either. In my head they feel more like a plea than a fact. *I hope it's nice and dry on the train. Please let us get her back.*

Eleazar wipes big drops of rain off his cheeks as we trudge through my neighbor's lawn.

My house is made of tan brick, like most houses on our street. I wonder if Eleazar's is the same. The paint on the windowsills is peeling very slowly, like an immortal snail has been cursed to make his way across our house for all eternity, breaking off tiny flecks of paint with his mucus and slime.

We walk through my door and are greeted with the smell of Fanksgiving—sweet potatoes drenched in cinnamon and maple syrup, slices of turkey smothered in fresh green herbs, a big ham with a brown-sugar glaze, and cornbread made from cornmeal that Mom grinds herself. It's the middle of April, but Mom makes Thanksgiving dinner whenever someone is having a bad day or a hard day or a day that's just different from all the other days. I call it *Fanksgiving* because it's fake Thanksgiving—and that's also how I used to pronounce *Thanksgiving*. Mom says it's because we always have something to be thankful for, but secretly I think it's because she gets tired of zucchini noodles too.

Mom and Dad smile from behind the island when we walk inside. Our kitchen and living room are sort of the same room. There's a couch wedged right under the kitchen island. Dad pokes a wood stick into the bottom of an apple and hands it to Mom. She dips it into a bowl of thick, smooth caramel. Mom makes candy apples instead of pie sometimes—she says handheld desserts are cuter and require less gluten.

Eleazar stands slightly behind me, his arms hanging awkwardly by his sides. He copies me and takes off his shoes when I take off mine, and sets them neatly on the mat by our door, but he still seems a little uncomfortable. I guess I'd feel the same if I were in a new person's house. I might not even get to the shoes-off stage.

Mom and Dad look surprised to see that I've brought someone home. Maybe they're uncomfortable too. Mom sets down the apple she was about to dip in caramel.

She signs, "How are you?"

"Good," I sign. Then I say out loud, "This is Eleazar. His dog ran away, and I'm going to help him look for her tomorrow. And I'm getting really good at Google Translate," I say, holding up my phone. "Did you know Google speaks Spanish, too?"

Dad raises an eyebrow. He's so bad at technology.

"Where's the last place you saw the dog?" Mom asks. I think she's talking to Eleazar, but my phone picks up her words. And since Eleazar looks too uncomfortable to speak, I respond.

"Down the street," I say. "By the train station. Can we go in the morning?"

Mom frowns. I hold up my phone so she knows to talk into it. "I'd go with you, but I'm teaching an art class in the morning, and Dad has to catch up on some work." She pauses. "I'm not sure if you should go alone. Wouldn't you rather spend your weekend resting?"

The station is only down the street—my parents usually let

me walk farther than that. But they're both acting so weird. I can't believe Dad is helping Mom make candy apples on his mental health day. Usually he'd be watching his shows or stealing my comic books to read.

"Please, Mom, it's really important. Eleazar's an artist too. We might work on a story together after."

Mom sighs. She exchanges a glance with Dad, which is not allowed in our house. My parents say that I should say what I mean and mean what I say, even though that's really hard to do. Something must really be wrong if they're giving each other secret looks.

"If you go, don't run near any cars," says Mom. "And there are more thunderstorms in the forecast for tomorrow."

"We know better than to chase a dog across the street, Mom," I say. "We're twelve."

She turns to Eleazar.

"Sorry to learn about your dog. Want to stay for dinner tonight?"

I feel my stomach growl. I look at Eleazar—he takes a big whiff of the food and nods.

"We can eat and work on our plan," I suggest. "Thanks, Mom. I mean *fanks*."

Her earrings dance a little when she nods, but worry lines her forehead. Mom wants me to be brave, but she needs me to be safe. I know she's afraid of what will happen if I get dizzy when I'm all alone. *But I'm not dizzy.* And I'm not alone, either. Besides, I know what to do when vertigo hits. I'll be okay. I grab a tissue from the table and hold it up to my nose for a few seconds longer than I need. The soft paper flutters up and down as I breathe deep.

Mom writes down Eleazar's mom's number.

"I'll go upstairs and give her a call real quick," she says into my phone.

Dad leaves a few pots simmering on the stove, then disappears upstairs with her. Eleazar and I sit down at our table, and I try not to worry about what my parents are going to say to each other. "Sure it's going to be okay for you to stay for dinner?" I ask Eleazar. He seems a lot more comfortable now that it's just us again.

"Definitely. My mom is so busy that she may not eat until

late. The last couple of days she's been stressed. She who is because all her college students are acting weird and my little sister spends her time waking up at night."

I ignore the translation errors and think about how stressed my own mom was yesterday. She was in the studio all day, and she didn't get anything done. "My mom's been acting strange this week too," I say.

"Do you think it's the storms?" he asks.

My ears ring worse when I expect them to start ringing. Like now. But I can't help it. Mom did say the weather was getting into her bones. If Eleazar is right and the train is the reason for the storms, and Mom's artist's block, and the city-wide curfew . . . I grit my teeth. Invincible Girl wouldn't let that happen. But she's not here. And if the CTA lady wouldn't listen to us, I'm sure no other adults will either. Mom and Dad would try to believe me, but they'd be so scared that they'd never let me go look for Louisa—and that's not an option. I made a promise.

I look at Eleazar. It's up to us to figure out what's going on.

Eleazar sets his stuffed messenger bag on the table. There's a corner of a book peeking out of the flap, but it's not his sketchbook. I point to it.

He takes the book out reluctantly and shows it to me. The cover says *Mujercitas*, and below that is the name *Louisa May Alcott*.

I type the word into my phone. Sure enough, it translates to *Little Women*.

"My grandma gave me this book when I left home," he says. "It's her favorite. And when Mom finally agreed to adopt a dog, Grandma called to tell me to name it something special. So Louisa became Louisa."

He stares out my kitchen window.

"So, um, you said Louisa is your best friend?" It's a weird question, but I don't know what else to say.

Eleazar says something into the phone, which is set on the table between us, then deletes it before I can read the words on the screen. He starts again.

"Yes," he says. "My little sister is cute, but she's only two. So now mostly I play with Louisa."

Now. That must mean something's different from how it

was before, like it is for me with the Quiet and the maybe-diagnosis.

I say, "Are your other friends still in Colombia?"

He shrugs like he doesn't want to talk about it. "Last week I saw you wearing headphones in the cafeteria. You were dancing. How can you hear music?"

He puts his hands over his ears and shakes his head to an invisible beat. *Oh no.* Sometimes when I listen to music, I start dancing and don't even realize what I'm doing. It's one of my worst habits. I fight the urge to run upstairs and lock myself in a closet. Actually, I don't move a single muscle. I don't want him to think I'm dancing again.

"Some days I can hear," I say. "Some days I can't. I can read people's lips a little bit when they're looking at me. But the phone works pretty well, right?"

Eleazar nods. "Yeah, it's cool. Do you know sign language, too?"

"Only a little," I say. "I'm learning now."

"Can you teach me? Maybe we will need a third language on the train."

"Oh! Really?" I smile. "I can try. I don't know if I'll be a good teacher, though."

I get too excited and my words squish together. I look down at my phone screen. Google Translate thought I said, "I doughnut Newfoundland beetroot preach cheerio."

Eleazar frowns at the translator.

"Um, how about I teach you the sign for *confused*? It's what I say to my teacher when she's signing really fast."

He nods. I touch my forehead with my right index finger, then I bring my palms in front of my body so that they face each other but don't touch. I move my hands together in a circular motion and raise one of my eyebrows so my face looks confused too.

"Confused," I say. I bend my finger again. Eleazar does the same.

"What should we say if we find Louisa?"

"Well, that would be *awesome*," I say. I teach him one of the first signs I learned for *awesome*. I put my thumbs over the tips of my middle fingers while the rest of my fingers are straight, and then flick my middle fingers upward. "This sign can mean *awful*, too. You just have to make a gross face."

Eleazar signs *awesome, awful, awesome, awful*. His face goes from happy to disgusted and back again. I laugh. He smiles for a second too, then looks away.

"Maybe one more?" I ask, hoping to cheer him up.

"How about *run*?" he asks. "In case we need to go fast."

"You can just pump your arms like you're running," I say. He pretends to run and makes me laugh again. "Are you really Spider-Man? How did you run so fast this morning?"

The translator changes Spider-Man to Hombre araña. Eleazar raises his eyebrow, and then he pretends to shoot webs over the table. This time when he laughs, he puts his hands on his stomach and throws his head back so hard that the piece of hair in his face flies backward. *I definitely cheered him up*, I think. I still don't understand why he just won't admit that he's worried. I guess it won't matter if we get Louisa back tomorrow.

"I'm not Spider-Man," Eleazar says. "But I like your comics. You're cool."

As the words pop up on the screen, he nods definitively, as

though that's the end of that, and for the rest of my days I'll now wear a sign that says HERE IS A GIRL WHO WAS ONCE DEEMED COOL.

He then becomes very interested in the tablecloth.

"Should we make a plan?" I ask. "I can do some research about trains if you want to make a list of stuff we'll need."

I search Google for *luminescent train, magic carpet train,* and *flower train,* but the best thing I find is a pretty picture of a train car filled with fresh flowers. I don't see anything that explains where the train came from—or why, even now, I get the feeling that it wants me to find it again. The words on my phone blur together as my head spins. I've barely ridden regular trains. Now I'll have to get on one that shouldn't exist.

I look for info on the train lines in Chicago.

Some of them were built for the World's Columbian Exposition in 1893, but Columbia with a *u* is apparently different from Colombia with an *o*, where Eleazar's from. *Are trains different in Colombia?* I don't know anything about his old home.

My phone says the Republic of Colombia has a population

of more than forty-nine million people. It's one of the world's most megadiverse countries and has the second-highest bio-diversity in the world, which I guess means there are animals other than squirrels and pigeons there. Maybe Eleazar has been to the Tropical Andes mountains. The most mountain-ous things I've ever seen are the sand dunes at the South Shore beach. Other than that, it's just the lake and all the tall, jagged buildings sitting side by side downtown.

I'm not sure any of this is useful, but I make some notes just in case. Eleazar's list looks almost done.

I hold my phone above the list so Google Translate can scan it. Good thing Eleazar's handwriting is neat and boxy—my app picks up the English translations right away.

Cosas que necesitamos / Things we need

Mapa de las líneas del tren / Map of the train lines

Galletas de perro / Dog biscuits

Pasaporte / Passport

El teléfono de Etta / Etta's phone

Dinero / Money

There's no way we need a passport. There must be

something wrong with the translator, but everything else seems okay.

"I can bring my phone tomorrow," I tell him. "I'll make sure I charge it tonight."

"I have money," says Eleazar. "In case we get lost and need to take a taxi."

I hope that he can't hear the THWACK-THWACK that pounds in my heart at the thought of getting lost downtown.

"Is that all we need?" I ask him.

"I think so." Eleazar's leg bounces up and down on our carpet. I bet he wishes he could do something more *now*. So do I. I feel like our list should be way longer. I don't have a plan for what to do if the train doesn't show up, or if Louisa's not on it anymore. I feel silly for expecting magic to be predictable, when everything I've read about it tells me we're in for a big surprise.

This is an *Adventure* with a capital *A*. It means my pages won't stay blank. I should be excited.

But as soon as I think about Adventure, the ringing in my ears and the memory of my doctor's lips spelling out the maybe-diagnosis fill my mind with doubt again. I look up at Eleazar and blink away a wave of dizziness.

I wish I could tell the nervous, fidgety Etta to go hide somewhere else for a little while. She whispers that adventures and new friends are not good ideas for Quiet Days—that magic is best when trapped inside books, and fireworks should stay in Indiana.

My headache agrees with the nervous Etta, and my mom probably does too. She'll want to know whether I've been feeling dizzy.

My maybe-diagnosis is an earthquake, shaking up my street and making it even harder for me to climb over the wall between me and my story. Invincible Girl could fly away from an earthquake, but if I'm ever going to escape, I need to start writing my way out now.

My parents come back into the kitchen. Dad carries platters of greens, turkey, ham, and sweet potatoes to the table. All the plates and platters are mismatched. Mom and I find them at thrift stores on dollar Saturdays. The best ones are always buried beneath the other stuff. They make Fanksgivings feel extra special. Mom brings some pieces of paper and a few pens to the table too.

On every Fanksgiving we play this game where we write down what we're most thankful for, and then the person sitting on our left has to guess what we wrote. Mom always says the game is "good for learning about gratitude and good for learning about empathy," right before she eats a piece of pineapple off the brown-sugar ham.

Fanksgiving is almost as good as writing at making the THWACKs get smaller. The best of both worlds is drawing a pile of sweet potatoes so high that you can barely see the turkey behind it. And then eating them in real life, of course.

Mom puts her mouth way too close to the microphone on my phone while she explains our thank-you game to Eleazar.

"I'll go first," she says, scribbling on her piece of paper. She looks at me. "Well, what do you think I'm thankful for?"

"Easy," I say, just as Dad's lips say the exact same words. "Sweet potatoes."

"And me," I add. Mom shows me her paper. I was right.

Eleazar leans forward to look at the sweet potatoes.

"It was Etta's grandma's recipe," says Mom. She laughs. "Actually, most of this food is somebody's grandma's recipe."

Eleazar sits back immediately. A dark shadow falls across his face.

"Uh, want to go next?" I ask him, but my voice falters halfway through and my words come out in one big nervous mumble.

The screen on my phone reads, "Onion wonton go flex?"

Oh no. I fight the urge to throw my phone into the garbage.

I turn the phone off and push a piece of paper into Eleazar's hand so he can write down what he's thankful for.

He looks at the paper like he's not sure what to do next. Then he looks up at me. In books they always use eye contact to speak in full sentences, like, *She gave him a look that clearly said,* If you ever touch my sandwich again, I'll hunt you down mercilessly.

It's amazing. Like, there's even an *adverb* in that sentence! And they always say it *just with their eyes.*

I stare straight at Eleazar now, hoping to see a sentence in his eyes, but I have no idea what he's trying to tell me.

He says something quickly before pushing his chair back and running for the door.

"Wait, what?" I say. I look at Mom. "What'd he say?"

Mom says, "He said he was late and had to go home. He said he was sorry."

"Maybe he doesn't like greens," says Dad.

Mom shushes Dad with her finger. "Everybody likes greens."

Maybe it *was* our food. Or the game. I try to remember if I said something wrong. Maybe my mumbled words translated into something offensive.

Or maybe he just didn't want to be here with me. *Does he still want to meet at the train?*

Mom sets a small plate of greens, macaroni and cheese, and sweet potatoes in front of me. She knows I like sides best. She even made a tray of gluten-free, low sodium macaroni and cheese just for me. After we got the maybe-diagnosis, when Mom said, *I'm feeling like a little dressing and cornbread,* I decided that I'd make all my Quiet Days my best days ever, like she does when she makes Fanksgiving on hard days. I'd wait to join basketball on a Quiet Day. I'd read up high in a tree on a Quiet Day. I'd make all my friends on Quiet Days. I'd chase magic and write the best story ever on a Quiet Day. *And how's that going for you, Etta Johnson?*

My head THWACKs.

"I think I'll take some food upstairs and go to bed early," I say.

Mom and Dad exchange another secret look. There is *definitely* something strange going on with my parents. Mom puts her hand over mine. Reluctantly I turn my phone back on. I guess I'm not going to bed yet.

"Etta, you don't have to go search for the dog tomorrow. Maybe you should stay home and rest."

My ears ring. It hurts, and I fight to keep the tears behind my eyes from betraying me to Mom.

"I'm fine," I say. A wisp of purple steam rises from my plate. Has the magic made its way here, too, into my own kitchen? Maybe that's why everyone is acting weird. Only, it still seems like Eleazar and I are the only ones who've noticed. Dad keeps talking and doesn't mention purple steam at all.

"Actually, there are a few things we want to talk to you

about," Dad says. "We were doing some research today and—wow, this thing works really well."

He takes my phone and looks over the words he just spoke.

"Booga booga boo," he says. "Etta, look at this. It even knows *booga booga boo*."

I take my phone back. "I *know*. You were saying something?"

"Oh right." He gets up and grabs a stack of papers from the counter. *Oh no*. It's the research on Ménière's disease. I read the title of the first article. "Ménière's Disease and Vertigo in Children."

I frown. Only a few kids have Ménière's, and I got lucky enough to have it in both ears, which I guess makes me one in a million or something. But I don't feel special.

"It says you should avoid stress, or the vertigo could come back," says Dad.

"It's not stressful to make a friend," I say. I don't say anything about magic.

Mom cuts in. "But lost dogs and curfews and this weather. It's too risky."

I cross my arms. I don't know why Eleazar left. But I know I can't take back my promise just because he ran away. I'm going back to the train no matter what.

The tears in my eyes form a shiny wall between my vision and the real world. *I'm so sick of walls and barriers and Rivers of Allergies in my way.*

Maybe it won't even be Quiet tomorrow. My ears might clear up.

"Please let me go," I plead. I notice that the puffiness under Mom's eyes is still there. "Did you finish your painting?"

She stares at her plate. "I'll be honest, Etta. The last few days have been hard for me. I think I'm just sick of all this rain. Sometimes storms . . . they get inside. We all need the sun."

My heart aches. I would do anything I could to keep the storms away from Mom. I would learn to fly with no super-powers. I would stop the train from making fireworks. I *will* do everything I can. Tomorrow.

I put my hand on hers. "Don't be afraid. Everything will be okay."

Mom squeezes my hand. "I don't want any choice you ever

make to be governed by fear either. But I'll admit, I'm pretty nervous."

"We both are," says Dad.

I want to say, *Me too*, but I stay quiet.

"But you deserve more than that," Mom says. "You deserve more than fear."

She pinches her nose. The licorice smell is getting worse. Even Fanksgiving dinner can't mask it.

"We all need to fight a little harder," says Dad, before picking up a big forkful of mac and cheese.

Mom smiles. "And you just keep being you, Etta. So you never have to be afraid."

Dad smiles too. "Our She-Hulk's got a lot of fight in her."

I think my parents are talking more for themselves than for me, but I feel better anyway. I take a screenshot of our conversation.

"So I can go?"

They nod.

"Thank you," I say, but it's not just a thank-you—it's a promise.

Tomorrow I will fight a little harder.

CHAPTER 8

IN THE MORNING my ears are ready. They're begging for birds that chirp, alarm clocks that ring, and bacon that POPS as it sizzles. But the world is quiet again.

You've got to be kidding me, Etta Johnson's ears.

Three Quiet Days in a row? The River of Allergies rushes through my ears as fast as it did yesterday.

It could mean nothing. It might be Loud again tomorrow.

Or it could mean that all my days will be Quiet—forever.

I pick up my pillow and wrap it all the way around my face, so far that it flattens my hair. *Okay, I'll make a deal with you, ears. You can be Quiet, but NO ringing and NO dizziness. Deal?* My ears respond with a soft, high-pitched ding, like tinnitus is ringing a doorbell in my brain.

No deal.

This isn't the sort of Quiet I love. It's not Quiet at all. I close my eyes and think about my comic.

INVINCIBLE GIRL: RISE AND SHINE, I'VE GOT A TRAIN TO CATCH AND A LOT OF FIGHT IN ME!

I repeat Dad's words—*she's got a lot of fight in her*—over and over in my head, until I feel strong enough to get out of bed. The smell of bacon wafts upstairs, but it's mixed with something else.

Charcoal and licorice. The magical scent is strong. If the train is coming at the same time this morning, that means it'll be there soon. There's a small, achy part of my heart that doesn't believe it's coming at all. But I'll never know if I don't show up. *And I hate not knowing.*

My feet find the floor. I put on jeans and my Chance sweatshirt before running downstairs. I pull my phone off the charger—I'm going to need it today. That is, if Eleazar's still planning to meet me.

He will. He'd never abandon Louisa May Alcott.

Dad's in the kitchen, standing over the stove. The bacon on the griddle is shiny and crisp, smothered in Dad's brown-sugar baste. When I got the maybe-diagnosis, he started making his own bacon with big slabs of pork belly. He mixes a special spice blend into the baste. It tastes even better than store-bought bacon. I grab a piece from the plate next to the pan.

He winks and scribbles in his notebook, *No salt. Extra sugar.*

A stack of papers on the table catches my eye.

Dad watches the direction of my gaze. I turn on my Google Translate so he doesn't have to write, even though I should probably save my battery for Eleazar.

"Mom printed these for you," he says.

> *LOST DOG*
>
> *NAME: LOUISA MAY ALCOTT,*
>
> *GOLDENDOODLE*
>
> *IF FOUND, PLEASE CONTACT ALVIRA*
>
> *JOHNSON (800) 555-0101*

"How did she know Louisa's name?"

"She called Eleazar's mom again. She said you could go to

their house for lunch too. After you put up the signs."

Mom believes in me so much that she did all this work to help. I look up the stairs and think about running up there to give her a big hug. Dad's eyes are on me. "I wouldn't go up to the studio now. She said she's determined to make something happen today. Something good."

"Me too," I say.

Dad sets a big roll of tape next to the stack of papers.

"Be safe when you go outside, Etta," he says. "Text us. I want you home before that new curfew starts at eight. Actually, you'd better come back at five just to be safe."

I flip over one of the flyers and scribble a note for Mom to read when she comes downstairs. I write, *Love you-love you.*

Because once is not enough.

Dad hands me the rest of the papers, but his fingers shake so much that I think he won't be able to hold on for long. It's weird to see him so nervous. I tell myself it will be okay. I'll figure out what's going on. For him and Mom.

"I feel great," I assure him. "I'll be home on time. See you soon."

I wish *great* wasn't a lie. The guilty feeling of it makes my stomach ache, but the truth is that my head aches too, and my brain is full of worry about the train.

"Thanks for the bacon," I say, but I hope he sees the other sentences in my eyes, the ones that say, *Thanks for telling me I'm strong* and *I wish I were as brave as you* and *I love you-love you.*

I put my backpack on as I walk out, because I know I'm going to need my sketchbook and Invincible Girl to fight the THWACKs and the ringing flooding my ears. The door shuts behind me.

My heart is beating way faster than usual. The sky is thick and gray and stormy. Clouds swirl around the street like steam dancing above a simmering pot of greens, except the clouds aren't comforting and delicious. Big droplets of rain land in my hair and stay there. I put my hood up and make sure my backpack is zipped tight.

It's so dark out, it feels like nighttime already. I hope we find Louisa soon. I reach the bottom of the stairs at the train station.

According to the time on my phone, the fireworks should be going off right about now. But I don't see them.

There might not be another train coming. Or worse—it left without me.

I climb the steps up to the station. Eleazar is there. We're the only two people on the platform again, but I'm too relieved to see Eleazar to think much about it. I set my stack of papers on the ground so I can pull out my phone.

"You came," he says. He looks surprised.

"I said I would."

Eleazar nods and stares at the empty space in front of him. "Thanks," he says. "Sorry I left."

I want to ask him why he ran out so quickly last night, but I'm worried he'll get upset. Instead I smile so he knows I don't need an apology.

"My phone is fully charged," I say. "And I grabbed some money, too. Look at these posters my mom made. We don't have time to hang them around the neighborhood, but they're pretty cool. Maybe—"

WHOOSH! A gust of wind stronger than a giant's punch

blows over the stack of papers at my feet. I see the words *LOST DOG* fly over the platform and settle on the train tracks below.

"No!" I cry. I know we probably weren't going to use them, but they did mean something—my mom believes in me. I walk to the edge of the tracks to see if there's one within reach. The rails turn gold. I startle backward, but a rush of excitement flows through me.

The train—*our train*—approaches, blowing deep purple smoke that sparks with shimmers of blue and white. The light on the front flicks on and off, like a blinking eye searching for its passengers. *For us.*

Purple sparks fly from the rails onto the platform as the train comes to a sudden stop in front of us. One of the sparks burns a small hole in my sweatshirt. The flowers on the side of the train are in full bloom, like a living mural graffitied onto the dark metal. An explosion of fireworks bursts into the sky.

Next to me Eleazar takes two steps toward the last car. The door at the end of the train opens again, and the carpet rolls out at our feet. The sign reads BOARDING. I see nothing inside, only a soft blue light.

Eleazar moves toward the door. When he looks over his shoulder, I see that his lips are moving, but his words aren't appearing on my phone. He's too far away.

"Wait!" I shout. "I can't understand you."

Frustrated, I shove my phone in my pocket. I wish we had a better way to talk to each other. My feet start to move too, but there's a sharp THWACK in my head. My vision goes blurry. I pause. I can't freeze again, but my feet are already so heavy. The feeling weighs me down, but something more powerful urges me forward. I *need* to do this. I can't just stay home, staring at the blank pages in my sketchbook and waiting for the storms to ruin everything—and I'm more afraid of that than I am of magic trains.

But I am afraid of both. I fight a strong urge to turn around and run home. What kind of hero runs before her story even starts? It's not like I have to fight some terrifying archnemesis or a dragon or my archnemesis's dragon or anything. Just a soft purple carpet. Like a welcome mat.

INVINCIBLE GIRL (WIPING HER SHOES ON THE CARPET): GOTTA HAVE CLEAN KICKS BEFORE YOU CONQUER THE WORLD.

Eleazar beckons for me to join him; then he disappears into the blue light beyond the train door.

The door fades in and out of my vision. This is my chance to have a story—*a Grand Adventure*—and make sure I don't fade away like muffled sounds and blank pages left on a train.

I can't leave Eleazar to find Louisa alone. I can't let Mom live with a storm in her bones. I made a promise to them both. I'm going to figure out why the clouds are coming from the smokestack and bring back the sun.

My feet break into a run. I cross the platform in long, leaping strides. I can almost see myself in the moving colors on the side of the train—soaring through the air like a superhero. My foot touches the carpet, I propel forward into the train car, and the door slides shut behind me.

ALL ABOARD.

I'm on the train.

CHAPTER 9

THE TRAIN ROCKS back and forth. I bump into Eleazar, who's still standing right by the entrance. We're moving, heading for the Loop. I try to ignore the shaky feeling of the train and focus on my surroundings.

The sliding door I came through is made of black glass. The floor of the train car is the same—slick and reflective like a mirror.

The blue light is more of a haze, thick and almost sticky. I run a finger over my sweatshirt to see if whatever's in the air is stuck to me, but my shirt is dry. My hair is dry too. The smells that came from the storm are even stronger in here—licorice and charcoal plus something too sweet, like strawberries sitting out on the counter for too long.

It's hard to see through the haze, but the train car seems small and narrow. There are no seats for passengers or boxes full of cargo. Louisa wouldn't have stayed in this train car for long. Shivers run through me—even though I'm on board, I still feel the pull of the train, like it wants us to keep moving. I think of the purple clouds pumping out of the smokestack. We have to find out how to stop them. But there's nothing here except blue haze and the dark, dark glass. I turn toward the door that leads to the front of the train.

A hundred white slivers of light snake across its surface.

I jump back. The door to the rest of the train—where Louisa must be—is covered in tiny white lines that squiggle and curl over the glass. They remind me of videos of parasites we watch in science class. *Yuck.* I shiver and look away.

Eleazar's orange hoodie sticks out in all the blue. It casts a warm orange glow over the dark glass floor, like we brought a little bit of sun in with us. I wonder if getting onto the train together makes us officially friends.

Friend feels heavier than other words, because when you have a friend, you're supposed to carry all this weight and knowledge about them, I think, like why they always wear an orange sweatshirt and what kind of comics they want to draw.

If we become friends, Eleazar will carry things for me too. I remember the promise I made to him and hold on to the brand-new feeling of his name.

Eleazar. Two *e*'s and two *a*'s, just like *Laureatte*.

Friend may be a heavy word, but *Eleazar* is a good name.

I pinch my nose to block out the old-strawberry smell and turn back to the white lines on the door.

They fold into more familiar shapes, shapes that make the next breath I take feel warm and comfortable. They're not parasites.

They're words.

The train is writing a poem for us. I always said I believed in the sort of magic you find in books, but I never believe-*believed* until now.

> *All are welcome, all aboard.*
> *Here you'll find all wishes stored.*

The Great Conductor welcomes you.
Find him in the engine room.

In nine train cars, have fun and play.
Find the clues along the way.
If you make it through each door,
All you wish for will be yours.

I open my mouth, but some of the blue haze settles on the tip of my tongue before I can say anything to Eleazar. It may smell strange, but it tastes *amazing,* sweet and pure like a blueberry candy cloud. *The Great Conductor welcomes you.* The words sparkle as I read them again. There's someone waiting for us. The conductor of a magical train. I wish I had a trampoline beneath my feet, because I feel like bouncing high. Until I turn and see Eleazar's lips moving. I didn't catch any of his words.

"Hold on," I say, sighing. "Let me get my phone out."

I'm so tired of trying to figure out what Eleazar meant to say every time my phone messes up. And it takes so much more time to talk. How are we going to find all the clues before curfew? I wish Ms. Suzy were here.

My phone screen is sticky with the blue haze. I rub it off with my thumb, but when I go to open Google Translate, the app isn't there. In its place is a new app that I definitely didn't download. It has a blue logo with the letters *MS* on it. I bite my lip and open it, hoping that it isn't a virus.

It looks almost like my Google Translate app, except at the top of the screen, above the language options, it says *Ms. Suzy*.

"We have to find the clues." Eleazar's words appear on the new app.

"Wait," I say. "Look at my phone. Can you repeat that?"

"I was saying, we have to find the clues," Eleazar says. "At least it's supposed to be fun. . . . Uh, Etta, why are you looking at me like that?"

"Because," I say excitedly. "This is a *magical* app. It's not Google Translate—see? It's named Ms. Suzy, like my live captionist. When you spoke, there were no mistakes. And it picked up all the punctuation too!" It's like Ms. Suzy is with me now, making sure I can understand everything.

Eleazar points to the line on the poem that says, *Here you'll find all wishes stored.* My magical app is definitely a wish fulfilled.

I smile as Eleazar touches his heart. "Louisa is what I want. She's all I want."

I look at the last line. *All you wish for will be yours.* But in order to get that, we have to make it through nine train cars. "You think Louisa made it all the way through?" I ask.

He nods. "She's good at sniffing out clues."

"Then we have to get to the engine room. If the storms are coming from the engine, then once we get there, we can stop those, too. The Great Conductor will be able to help us, right? Maybe he's already with Louisa."

Maybe. THWACK-THWACK. My head aches.

"Do you think the Great Conductor knows about the storms?" I ask.

For a moment Eleazar looks uncomfortable; then he shrugs. "Probably not."

I can just barely see my own reflection in the dark glass behind the train's poem.

My eyes are way too wide, probably because my brain

doesn't know whether to be scared or excited. And my mouth is hanging open.

Oh no, is my mouth always hanging open like that?

The rest of me looks okay: long-sleeved sweatshirt with a big number three in the middle, dark blue jeans, Jordans that Dad bought for my birthday.

My big puffs of tiny, coiled curls are half-hidden by the haze. I look pretty cool, like someone I would ask for help with something important. I've got to do more than look cool, though. There's a story here, in all this magic, and I'm going to figure out what it means.

I put one hand on the door, then freeze—I haven't gathered enough bravery to go on yet. This is where Invincible Girl would come to the rescue, all action and capital letters and flying through the door to start our adventure.

I take out my sketchbook and draw nine tiny train cars in a line. Then I draw the engine at the front of the train. Eleazar watches over my shoulder. Each train car I draw makes me feel a little more sure of myself. They're just little boxes with wheels. No big deal.

I hand my pen to Eleazar, and he sketches a little drawing of Louisa May Alcott at the very front of the train.

It looks like a long journey, but the poem says that wishes are stored here. The train cars are filled with *fun*. I already have a brand-new Ms. Suzy app. I can do this.

Suddenly the white letters on the door start to change. They stick together like melted marshmallows, then form a rectangle that solidifies. It looks almost like a mailbox hanging on the door, with a slot that tilts open. Eleazar sticks his hand inside before I can tell him to wait.

He pulls out a shiny white ticket. There are words printed on it in glittery purple ink: most of them are in Spanish, but I recognize his name. *Eleazar.* His hand trembles a little.

I step forward, take a deep breath, and place my hand inside the slot. There's another ticket there.

BOARDING PASS

Passenger: Laureatte Johnson, aka Etta

Destination: Undecided

Paid in Full OR Pays with Fuel

I grip the paper so tight that some of the ink rubs off on

my thumb. I have no idea how much a magical train ticket costs, what kind of fuel I should pay with, or how long it'll take to find the Great Conductor, but none of that matters. *The train knows my name.* I don't know who told it to call me *aka Etta*, but if I have a ticket, then I'm supposed to be here. I have to make a choice to go forward.

And all the way through the train. For as long as it takes to help Louisa and Mom.

Eleazar slides open the door and walks through in front of me.

I put the ticket in my pocket and wrap my arms around my middle.

There's a jar of courage inside my stomach, collecting butterflies and trapping them under a metal lid. Most days the lid pops open and the butterflies go flitting around, messing with my nerves, but I can't let that happen now. I screw the lid on tight.

CHAPTER
10

THERE'S A LIGHT above us, as big and bright as the sun. *Exactly* as big and as bright. It doesn't come from a bulb on the ceiling but from a wide expanse of blue sky, illuminated by a yellow-white circle in the distance. My heart is too stunned to THWACK. The world around us is just that—a whole world. It feels like we're standing outside, but we should be in the second train car. I could try to draw our surroundings in my sketchbook, but I'd never do it justice.

The sunshine and its shadows fall over green trees, gray buildings, and the smooth, rounded shape of mountains in the distance. We're standing on a patch of sand in the middle of some sort of park. The air is warm and thick with moisture. It's nothing like April in Chicago. I wipe a bead of sweat off the back of my neck. There are so many feelings inside me, pushing at the edges of my heart and my brain. A rising sense of panic, a feeling of wonder so strong that I think I could fly. I don't know how to handle them all at once. Then I look up, at the blue sky. And I breathe deep.

The ground vibrates beneath my sneakers. *Weird.* I kneel down and put my hand on the sand. I feel a steady rumbling, like a train rattling over its tracks. *A train!*

We haven't left Chicago. We're just standing in a train car with no ceiling, no walls, and no door to get through to the other side. I spin around. The door we came through disappeared too.

My heart pounds in my chest. THWACK-THWACK. *We're stuck here.* I stare at the cloudless sky again and breathe through the fear pounding in my chest. There's got to be a door here somewhere; we just need to find the clues first, like the poem said.

For a moment I wonder whether this is a vacation train, like a cruise ship for people from Chicago, tricking everyone and their winter blues into believing they're somewhere warm. But there aren't any other people here. Instead there are rectangular columns planted in the park. They're made of gray stone, and they're scattered across the sand. They look like steps, but they're all out of order. Some of them are only as tall as my ankles. Others reach almost all the way up to the sky.

I lift my face to the sun. It feels nice, but this is all so strange. Summer's still a long way away. I look at Eleazar and sign one of the words I taught him: *Confused.*

He doesn't look like he feels confused. He has the goofiest smile on his face.

Eleazar's lips move quickly. I pull out my phone, and he takes a deep breath, slowing down for the translator even though I'm pretty sure my magical new app can handle him talking fast.

"This is Medellín," he says.

"What is Med—" I pause. I wouldn't be sure how to pronounce the word even if I could hear myself talk. I close my mouth.

"The City of Eternal Spring," he says. "My city. I'm home."

"In Colombia? But . . . this is Chicago. I think we're still on the train."

And Chicago is both of our cities. *Isn't it?*

Eleazar frowns and looks around. "Doesn't look like Chicago."

"But can't you feel that we're still moving?"

He shrugs and points toward the mountains. "My grandma lives that way. We can go see her! Can you believe it?"

"No, I can't," I say. I'm not sure I want to.

Eleazar jumps off the patch of sand and plants his feet on the concrete.

"Wait," I say. "Is the park usually this empty?"

Eleazar looks around. There are no people here. No cars moving on the street behind the park, and no birds flying around in the sky.

"It's a fake," I say. Like Fanksgiving. *Fedellin.* "We shouldn't go much farther."

Eleazar frowns. "You think the clue is here?"

"Why else would the train door lead right to the park?"

He stares at the mountains again.

"What about Louisa? She probably ran off."

"I bet she wouldn't have been able to get far. It's all some sort of trick, don't you think?"

"Then where is she?"

"I don't know," I say, my heart sinking. "You said she was smart. Maybe she found the way into the next train car."

Eleazar's chest falls as he sighs.

"But do you think this train goes to Medellín, or what? How else could it know what the city looks like?" he asks.

I shake my head quickly and swallow my panic. *This train better not go to another country.* "It just goes around Chicago, right? I don't think any train goes that far. . . ."

My words catch in the back of my throat.

Eleazar stares at me, but I can't read the sentence in his eyes. His fingers twitch.

Eventually he shrugs. "It just looks so much like Barefoot Park. I thought . . . my grandma . . . but I guess it's just Chicago."

Just Chicago. I let out a deep breath and read the Spanish side of my Ms. Suzy app. We're standing in the Parque de los Pies Descalzos, or at least the train's version of it.

"I know you're probably disappointed," I say, trying to hide my own relief. "But we should focus on getting to the engine room."

Eleazar puts on his goofy smile again, but he doesn't meet my eyes.

"I'm not disappointed. This is fun." He bends down and unties his shoes.

"What are you doing?" I ask.

"You're supposed to take your shoes off and relax. I'm going to climb up on the columns. Maybe when I'm up there, I can see what we're supposed to do next. I can see how far the city goes."

I frown at my sneakers. I'm not sure how I'm supposed to relax when a park from another country magically shows up on a CTA line. But toes in the sand . . . that might actually be nice.

Eleazar stares at me expectantly.

I sigh, kick my shoes and my socks off, and toss them into my backpack.

He winks at me, and I roll my eyes. Eye rolling is the only appropriate response to winking.

Eleazar steps onto one of the ankle-high columns. "When I was little, the columns looked so big. I would pretend I was Spider-Man and could shoot webs that would help me fly between them."

He steps up to reach a knee-high column near him. As he moves, a thin white string falls from the sky. He grabs it as his feet land on the second column.

It's strong enough to hold him up. He spins around to face me. His shocked expression is so funny, he might as well be a comic book character. A little bit of his scream bursts through the River of Allergies in my ears. I don't think there were magical strings falling from the sky at the real park in Colombia. My heart swells in awe and THWACKs with a too-good-to-be-true warning at the same time.

I look up, but I can't see where the string is coming from. The sun is too bright. *Maybe the train car does have a ceiling, and we just can't see it.* That means there's a door here somewhere too.

"Wait!" I call out. "There's a clue here, remember? Do you see anything weird? I mean, besides the string hanging from the sky."

But instead of looking at the columns or the park around us, Eleazar stares far into the distance. His feet wobble as he tries to stay balanced, but the magical string keeps him steady. "I think I can see my grandma's street! And Louisa's favorite bakery!"

The clue must be close by, but Eleazar can't seem to focus.

He needs my help. I ignore the sand stuck between my toes, put my phone in my pocket, and step onto the small column. Eleazar reaches his hand out to pull me up to the higher column, but I reach for the string in his hands instead. It feels sticky. Eleazar lets go, and I grab on to the string with both hands. "Do you see any clues on the columns?" I ask. I stop to catch my breath after every word because I'm focusing so hard on staying balanced.

Eleazar turns away from the city and focuses on the columns. The one closest to him is taller than my dad and at least five feet away, but he leaps for it anyway. Another string falls from the sky while he's in midair. He grabs it and swings up onto the column. He plants one foot on the column and grins at me.

He has a few things that I maybe don't have as much of: trust, courage, *fearlessness*.

I pull down on the string in my hands and slowly lift my feet off the column. My body hangs in the air, and the string spins me around slowly.

I might be the world's worst Spider-Girl, but still—*I'm hanging in midair!* I can almost see myself on a page in a comic book, holding on for my life.

Eleazar keeps swinging from column to column. He is almost at the other side of the park now. I set my feet back on the column and pull my phone out of my pocket carefully.

"What are you doing?" I ask. "What about the clue?"

"If I can see my grandma's street, then maybe she's there. Maybe it's real."

"No, Eleazar—wait!" He takes a giant leap forward, trying to swing over two columns at once. He looks even more like a hero swinging over the columns than he did running after the bus. Then the string snaps and he crashes onto the sand. *Ouch.* I wonder how often Spider-Man falls like that.

INVINCIBLE GIRL: AND THIS IS WHY I CHOOSE TO FLY INSTEAD OF WEB AROUND LIKE A SPIDER.

"Are you okay?" I ask. He sits up and rubs his back, frowning at the broken string in his hand.

The sand moves beneath him. The bottom of his messenger bag disappears, and then his feet do too.

"Eleazar, you're sinking!"

He scrambles to get up, but his feet only sink farther into the sand, until he's buried all the way up to his knees.

His lips move fast. Ms. Suzy's app is blank.

"Wait!" I call out. "Can you talk louder? My phone can't hear you."

He tries again.

"Help! Swing over to me and pull me out."

I shake my head. I can barely balance on this column as it is.

"You can do it," he says.

"Eleazar, I am *not* about to just leap across," I say. "Look what happened to you!"

"That's because I tried to leap over too many at once. When I was little, my grandma used to get mad when I tried to jump too far. I'm a bobo."

His last word doesn't translate. I frown at the Ms. Suzy app.

"I don't know what that means," I cry out. Fear THWACKs in my chest.

I can't do this. I don't know how I ever thought I could. I'll fall and sink into the sand with Eleazar. I should have stayed home and rested like Mom wanted.

Only, Mom didn't really want me to stay. She made the LOST DOG signs for me. I remind myself that I'm here for her.

So blank canvases and blank pages don't stay blank.

Eleazar looks at me desperately. "Please . . . I trust you."

Trust is a word as heavy as *friend*, big enough to bring you crashing down from the sky. But it's big enough to hold on to you too.

I place my hand on the column closest to me. There's something inscribed on the side that I didn't notice before.

"Wait, Eleazar, there are words here! I think I found the clue!"

His eyes widen with excitement as he sinks farther into the sand. "Maybe it can help you get across!" he says. "What do you see?"

"Um, it's in Spanish. There's like a little squiggly line on the top, and then some words."

I scan the words into the Ms. Suzy app and press the speaker button so Eleazar can listen as I read.

~

De lejos vengo,

muy lejos voy,

piernas no tengo, viajero soy.

~

From far away I come,

Very far away I go,

Legs I do not have, a traveler I am.

Eleazar scrunches his eyebrows together. "I think I've heard that before."

"Do you know what it means?"

"Give me a minute to think," he says, but I'm not sure he has that much time.

"Someone from far away," I say. "A traveler. What about you? You traveled from far away."

"I have legs, though," says Eleazar. He looks down at the sand rising up to his waist. "Usually."

"Something that comes and goes, then," I say. "Like an airplane or a bus or a train. They all go both ways, right?"

"That's it!" says Eleazar excitedly. "Well, no, it's not any of those things. It's just the way. The path. A path doesn't have legs, but it travels far. You have to follow the path."

I read his last word in Spanish. *Camino* means *path*. I look more closely at the columns to try to decide which direction I should go in. Some of them have the same ˜ sign engraved on the side.

"There are little signs on some of them. Do you think that's the path?" I ask.

Eleazar nods. "Follow them one by one. Don't jump around like I did."

I think of the columns like comic book panels. You can't skip around when writing comics. If you miss a panel, you lose a part of the story. They all fit together . . . like pieces of a puzzle.

Eleazar has sunk down to his shoulders. I step carefully to the closest column bearing a ˜, and then to the next.

"That's it!" says Eleazar. "That's how my grandma told me to do it. One at a time."

New strings fall from the sky as I move. Small leaps carry me across the sand, until I'm standing on a short column right above Eleazar.

He wrenches one of his arms out of the sand and reaches up. I slip my phone into my pocket so I can grab him with both hands.

"Trust me," I say. Now that we've each said it once, the word feels even heavier.

I pull with all my might. Invincible Girl doesn't have to do push-ups to stay strong, but I probably should have tried harder in PE.

Eleazar emerges slowly from the sand, kicking until he's all the way out. As soon as he gets free, a door appears in front of us. It's shiny and silver and has a handle to slide it open.

Eleazar hops onto the column next to me and brushes sand off his clothes. "Thanks," he says. "I knew I'd get out."

His eyes are bright, and his fists are clenched. If Invincible Girl lost all her powers and became a regular kid, I bet she'd be confident like Eleazar. I wonder if she'd be as secretive, too. I notice the beads of sweat on his forehead and the way his chest rises and falls with huge breaths. He must have been terrified, but he doesn't say anything. I follow his gaze over the mountains, into the bright blue and endless sky. He bends down and grabs a bunch of sand. It trickles from his fist, grain by grain, until his hand is empty. I try to imagine how hard it would be to say goodbye to a train car that looks so much like home.

I look for a sentence in Eleazar's eyes, but all that's there is the same almost-purple gleam I noticed in his eyes on the bus two days ago.

"Let's get Louisa," he says. I nod.

There's sweat dripping down the sides of my face. I realize that we didn't bring any water or food. We put passports on the list, but not water. *Great.* And as soon as I think about food, I feel my stomach rumble. One piece of Dad's bacon wasn't enough for this kind of adventure.

I put my shoes on slowly, trying to save my energy. It already feels like we've come so far. The path ahead is going to be a long one.

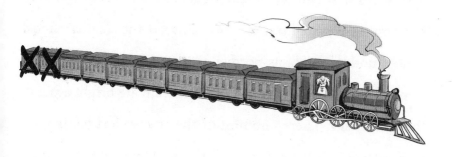

CHAPTER
11

WE STEP OUT onto a bridge between train cars. The door slides shut behind us, and Medellín disappears. From out here, on the elevated tracks above Chicago, the train cars look almost normal—well, as normal as magic train cars can get. The swirling colors on the sides of the train are bright against the stormy sky. There's no hint of the city we left behind, or of whatever is waiting for us in the next train car. I look at Eleazar and try to ask a question with my eyes—*What comes next?*—but I can tell he's still thinking about Medellín.

I focus on the door ahead. My arms feel weak and shaky,

and my stomach grumbles again. As I grip the handle, I wish for something that would make me strong.

The next train car doesn't have a city inside. Unless there's a city they don't teach about in schools that has lemonade stands instead of buildings, and flying caramel apples instead of airplanes and cars. Long lines of food stands extend through the car, and more colorful, edible things float around them, some near the ground and some zooming around above our heads. The sky is the color of orange soda, and it's covered in cotton-candy-blue clouds. The door we came through disappears just like it did in Medellín. Eleazar and I are left in the middle of a road with food stands lining either side. The road extends ahead of and behind us, as far as I can see. I don't see any people cooking or watching the stands, but I can smell fresh-baked brownies and roasting garlic.

A caramel apple as big as my head floats in front of my face.

I don't know what I expected to find when we opened the door, but it wasn't flying food. My rumbling stomach thanks me. *Here you'll find all wishes stored.*

"Hang on, Eleazar," I say. "When we were in the first train car, did you wish for home?"

He nods, even though he doesn't make eye contact. "Maybe. Why?"

"Because I was just thinking about how hungry I was. I think . . . I think I wished for this."

Eleazar looks impressed. "You made this train car?"

"I guess so."

I can't help but smile as a rainbow-colored lollipop zooms by. I grab it instinctively, and then let it go. It continues its happy zoom around the train car.

I look at Eleazar.

"Awesome," he signs.

"Awesome," I sign back. It's the only word we need right now.

The lollipop leads me on a tour. The food stands carry big platters of different types of food, and they have banners above them. Some of the banners describe the food underneath, and others are covered in long, hanging strands of Twizzlers or pictures of towers made out of cheese. Everywhere I look, food floats around the spaces between the stands like cars speeding along the highway. I feel the rumble of the train beneath us, keeping me tethered to my own world even as I explore this new one.

I don't see any zucchini noodles. This would be Mom's worst nightmare and Dad's favorite dream. But I'm not asleep. For me, it's all real.

All I want to do is stuff my face with food. Eleazar licks his lips and walks toward the stand that smells like fresh brownies. I wander in the other direction.

In front of a hot dog stand, I find two red bowls with white dog bones on them. One has a little bit of water in it, and the other has a smear of peanut butter inside.

"Look!" I call out. "If Louisa May found a train car like this, then that means she had plenty to eat and drink."

Eleazar rushes over to the bowls when he hears Louisa May's name. "She loves peanut butter. I bet she wished for all kinds of treats. If only she were here now."

I stare at his words on my phone screen. I don't know if he's happy that she's okay or sad that he can't watch her chase floating food around. I feel better knowing that Louisa's belly isn't empty after staying here all night, but she's probably lonely.

"We should focus on finding the clues," Eleazar says. Maybe he's worried about Louisa being lonely too.

"You're right," I say, even though I might be speaking more to my own stomach than to him. "I'm not allowed to eat most of this food anyway. Let's just find the riddle."

Eleazar nods, but when a bag of hot Cheetos floats in front of his face, he grabs it and rips it open. He eats a Cheeto and gives me the *awesome* sign again, even though he messes it up because he doesn't let go of the bag. My stomach growls. Maybe a quick snack doesn't count as a distraction. Especially not when I'm this hungry.

There's a stand to my left with a white banner and red letters.

peRfectly healthy RaspbeRRy popsicles

The *R*s are all capitalized, which is weird, but the inky letters are so bright, they look like they were made out of crushed raspberries. Beneath the banner is a white cooler full of red Popsicles.

Maybe *perfectly healthy* means that this won't affect me in any weird way. Magical food might not have the same rules as regular food. My stomach hurts again, but this time I'm not sure whether it's from hunger or guilt that I'm breaking Mom's rules.

Because I'm going to try a Popsicle.

Just one taste. After all, raspberries are a breakfast food, and Popsicles probably don't have salt in them. Invincible Girl would demolish this place. Superheroes have big appetites. How bad can it be to be brave for once?

I touch the Popsicle to my lips. *Not bad at all.* It's cold and refreshing and perfectly sweet.

Eleazar walks around to a few other food stands, probably looking for any more signs that Louisa's been here. I'm trying to refocus on finding the clue that'll unlock the door, when a thin, round thing that looks like a cookie smeared with caramel floats at the same height as Eleazar's mouth. He opens wide and catches the treat on his tongue.

"Eleazar!" I exclaim. The sight of him catching a cookie right in his mouth is so surprising that I drop my own Popsicle and laugh.

His cheeks redden, and he tries to say something with his mouth full. I look away so he can have a chance to chew.

The caramel apple that zoomed by earlier catches my eye again. It's so shiny.

I place a fingertip on the side of the apple, and it stops mid-zoom. The caramel is soft and warm, and the color is so perfect, a deep and glowing golden brown. A sticky pinch covers my finger. I take a little bite. It's buttery and not too sweet, with a hint of salt.

"Ohh," I breathe. All the books I've read have told me that magic would mean elves and supervillain sorcerers and animals that speak. I didn't know it would be delicious.

I haven't had much salt today. I should be able to eat a little bit more without anything bad happening.

THWACK-THWACK. I ignore the pounding in my head. I'm so hungry.

This train car is filled with all the salty foods I've missed. I assure myself there's such a thing as magic salt.

INVINCIBLE GIRL (FACING A MONSTER MADE OF SALT): THE ONLY WAY TO DEFEAT YOU . . . IS TO EAT YOU!

Eleazar is carrying a giant platter filled with steak and rice and a bunch of other things. It looks like he's picked up something from every food stand. When he sees me look at him, he offers a round disk to me and points at a nearby stand with a banner that says *vivan las aRepas*. The disk is almost like a burger bun but made out of something denser. The word he speaks into my phone is the same one on the banner—*arepa*—but it doesn't translate into English.

"Corn," he says. "And cheese."

I bite into it—slightly crisp on the outside, soft and cheesy in the middle. It's wonderful.

Arepa, with an *a* at either end. It's a good word.

Eleazar smiles.

"I've never seen these before," I say.

He takes my phone. "At home my grandma made them every day."

Home. He means Colombia again.

"You don't eat them here?"

He shrugs. "My mom's too busy to cook. And no one else in my class is Colombian."

I didn't realize he felt so alone too. He avoids my eyes and hands me other things that don't translate—patacones, crunchy chicharrón, and some kind of yummy breaded meat called mil-anesa. I add all these new foods to the weight of the word *friend*.

I share with him, too—a Chicago hot dog from a stand with a red-and-yellow banner, piled high with mustard, tomatoes, pickles, and neon-green relish; macaroni and cheese from a stand whose banner reads *sizzling soUl food*, just like the kind Mom bakes; and grits with mounds of sugar. Dad would not approve. He always gives me a crooked smile and then says, "How about some grits with all that sugar?" and tries to make me eat his savory grits. But I can't help myself.

"This is from this city?" Eleazar asks about the hot dog. He reaches for a ketchup packet.

Ketchup! On a hot dog? I snatch it from him. The words on the little package read: *Unbelievably scrUmptioUs all-natUral ketchUp.*

More capitalized letters. Everything we eat is steaming like it's fresh out of the oven, but there are no ovens and no chefs in sight. I wonder who made these stands and all this food. I turn to Eleazar to ask him, but as I do, a juice stand catches my eye.

I eat and eat, but my stomach isn't full. Platters of food

leave their stands like they have minds of their own and float toward us. Even the stands move closer and closer to us like we're honey; the food buzzes like bees around us. I grab a piece of deep-dish pizza floating over my left eye and take a quick bite before a big glob of cheese melts onto the ground. I haven't had pizza in over a year, and even then it was only the kind made with cauliflower crust.

I grab other things, too—sour cream and onion chips, a thick piece of garlic bread, and a miniature blueberry pie with whipped cream from a stand called *slice of heaveN pies 'N more*. My stomach feels bigger and hungrier the more I eat, like a treasure chest begging to be stuffed with more gold.

I savor every second that we spend wandering around the food stands. After all, if the Maybe turns into a For Real, I might not be able to eat food like this ever again. *Maybe this is the one and only time I'll get to try an arepa.* It's a sad and scary thought.

The world starts to spin around me. The colors on the food stand banners blur together.

No, no. Not here. Not now.

I drop the cinnamon roll in my hand and hold on to my ears,

trying to push away the ringing that fills them as the dizziness gets worse. I'm not sure if it's all the salt I just ate, or the salt on top of everything else. Invincible Girl might be able to defeat the salt monster, but Etta Johnson should have known better.

I focus on the red circle of a lollipop on the ground and take deep breaths. After a few minutes the spinning slows, but when I look up, Eleazar doesn't look the same. There are sprinkles on his nose, and his eyes are too wide and too gleeful, like a clown that takes its job too seriously and starts to look creepy instead of cheerful. He didn't even notice me sitting still—he's too busy eating.

The food made us forget all about Louisa, like some sort of salty illusion. It isn't helping us get to the next train car—it's *distracting* us.

My nose fills with the sudden smell of licorice and food that's gone bad. *Ugh!*

In front of me Eleazar spits out a mouthful of small round candies. They bounce and crash across the ground.

"Awful," Eleazar signs.

He picks up the wrapper from the candies and reads it.

"Disgusting," he says into my phone. "What's in this? Why are there capital letters in the middle of all the words? English is weird."

I lean over to look at the wrapper, but the giant candy apple I tasted earlier floats in front of me again. It turns brown and mushy and slides right off the stick, and lands in a smelly pile next to my sneakers.

My whole body shivers in disgust.

I turn back to Eleazar, and my hands fly to my mouth. Creepy, crawly gummy worms are pouring out from behind one of the food stands to form a pile around his feet. They climb up his legs, past his shirtsleeves, and onto his face.

"Eleazar, look!" His hands fly to his face, and he tries to pull a gummy worm off his cheek, but they're stuck to his skin like neon leeches.

Gah! Something pricks my ankle. A gummy worm is crawling up my right pant leg. As soon as I reach down to pick it off, another worm takes the opportunity to crawl into my other pant leg and pinches my skin.

There's a big jar of peanut butter sitting on the stand next to Eleazar, right by a leaking tub of jelly and a pile of moldy green bread.

When I got gum stuck in my hair in second grade, Mom used peanut butter to get it out. Maybe that'll work for leeches, too.

I take a big glob of peanut butter out of the jar with my fingers, cover one of the gummy worms with peanut butter, and try to loosen the edges. Then I pull until it POPs off my leg. It wriggles around in my fingers, trying to find something not peanut buttery to latch on to. I throw it as hard as I can at one of the stands, where it hits with a THWOP and then sticks.

Gross! All I want to do is sign *awful*, over and over again until all of this stops.

I peel another gummy worm off, but before I can throw it, it wraps around my pinky and squeezes tight.

It won't come off, so I put my finger in my mouth and bite right through the worm. I feel the sour crunch of something rotten between my teeth before spitting out the pieces.

Eleazar pries gummy worms off his arms and throws them as far as he can. I help him, kicking and smooshing the worms as soon as they fall to the ground. The food stands are splattered with the colorful worms, like a weirder version of the art you get to make in kindergarten with glue and macaroni noodles.

But as we fight, more and more sticky, rotten foods crawl toward us.

They're trying to trap us here. I imagine gummy worms and french fries crawling down my throat, drowning me in sugar and salt.

Another wave of dizziness washes over me. I focus on the peanut butter jar in my hands to steady myself.

Nothing better thaN peaNut butter.

More capital letters. A thought floats through my dizzy brain: "Eleazar, what did you say about capital letters?"

"I said English is weird," he says.

"English is weird," I agree. "But there aren't supposed to be capital letters in the middle of words."

"It's the clue!" he says.

I think of the capital letters on the other labels and food banners.

peRfectly healthy

ketchUp

peaNut

Oh no. "Eleazar, what are the capital letters on your wrappers?"

He pulls a gummy worm out of his ear, then runs around. He picks up random wrappers scattered around him as I look at the banners around us. The same three letters are capitalized, over and over again.

viva las aRepas

sizzling soUl food

slice of heaveN pies 'N more

U-N-R-R-N-U-R-U-N, Eleazar says.

R-U-N. R-U-N, I yell.

Eleazar looks up, horrified, and I follow his gaze. The gummy worms are getting tangled up with the other foods, squishing together, growing and growing into a monster that stands eight feet tall. It has a Flaming Hot Cheeto body, gummy worm legs, pepperonis for eyes, and long Twizzler fingers that reach out to grab me. I can imagine Invincible Girl kicking this thing right in the face, but I don't want pizza sauce on my shoes, and I'm pretty sure it'd eat my foot anyway. I'll save the kicking for my story.

"RUN!" I shout again.

A silver door appears just beyond a spaghetti stand a few feet in front of us—but the monster is right behind us. As Eleazar races toward it, a canister of whipped cream rolls by his feet. He grabs it and tosses it to me. I spray the candy monster's pepperoni eyes. Eleazar raises his fists as the monster blindly lunges toward us, but now is not the time to be fearless. We need to get out of here before Eleazar loses a hand to the monster's sharpened candy-cane teeth.

I jump over an old pizza box to reach him and press down on the door handle, ignoring the spaghetti squishing beneath my fingers.

I should have trusted the guilty feeling in my stomach. Mom's rules may not apply here, but the train's do.

And they aren't as friendly as I thought.

CHAPTER
12

WE SLAM THE door on the candy monster and run into the next train car. The ground beneath us is covered in small green and brown pebbles. They're as smooth as the pieces of glass that float around in Lake Michigan for too long. The pebbles form a long piece of a straight shoreline that covers all the ground behind us. All along the shoreline, and as far across as I can see, is a huge body of water. It must be bigger than Lake Michigan, because when Mom and Dad take me to the lake on a clear day, I sometimes think I can see all the way to the blurry shoreline on the other side. I don't see anything on the other side of the water here. It's like the train has its own ocean.

"Did you wish for this?" I ask Eleazar.

He shakes his head. "I wished for Louisa."

"Me too."

Here you'll find all wishes stored. What does it mean when neither of us get what we want? The Great Conductor and I have different definitions of *fun*. Small waves splash against the pebble-covered shore.

An eerie feeling settles over me. I look back over the water. There's something there—a shadowy shape floating on the waves.

I grab Eleazar's arm, but all he does is raise an eyebrow. I wish for once he would admit he is as worried as me. It makes me feel lonely to be the only one shaking in my sneakers. The shape in the water is far away, but as we stare, it gets bigger and bigger, until it becomes more rowboat-shaped than dark-blob-shaped. There's a girl inside who looks about our age. Eleazar waves his arms frantically.

"We don't know who that is!" I warn. He shrugs.

The boat runs into the pebbles, and the girl crawls out. Her legs are wobbly, like she's not used to solid ground. It reminds me of how I feel when I get vertigo.

She has light brown skin and long hair that's frizzy on the top and curly on the bottom. She looks at us curiously.

The skin around her eyes is red and puffy. She starts talking, but her lips are hard to read.

"Um, can you talk into my phone?" I ask her. "I'm—I can't hear you. Um, hearing loss. Sorry. It'll be able to hear you, so it's not that big a deal, I don't think. Uh . . . yeah."

I fumble with the Ms. Suzy app, then extend my phone to the girl so she can see the translator, not realizing that one of the nasty, nefarious gummy worms is still crawling over my screen. *Ugh!* I try to flick the gummy worm away, and drop my phone.

The girl's nose wrinkles, and she turns to Eleazar instead.

He says something. Probably his name. I try to jump back into the conversation.

"And I'm Etta."

I pick up my phone and turn on the microphone.

The girl says, "I'm Mariana. Who are you? What happened to you?"

She looks over our food-stained clothing.

"Didn't you just get attacked by food too?" I ask. "In the last train car?"

She frowns. "The train car before this one was made entirely of glass."

I guess that makes sense. If she didn't wish for food, she wouldn't have gone through the same car we did.

"The train changes?" Eleazar says. I'm not sure if he's asking a question or stating a fact.

"Of course," Mariana says. "But it isn't working right. I've been stuck in this train car for almost two days. It isn't supposed to be like this."

Now we're stuck in her wish too. Eleazar is talking to Mariana in English, but he stands next to me so he can double-check the translation over my shoulder. I feel glad that he used Spanish with me. It makes me feel like the phone is less of a barrier between our friendship and more our secret, special way of talking.

"Two days?" Eleazar asks. "Aren't you hungry?"

He picks up the gummy worm and extends it to her cautiously.

"Gross," she says. "I have plenty of food."

Mariana points to a big backpack in the boat. "I came to stay on the train. What are you all looking for?"

"We're here to find his dog, Louisa," I say. "And to figure out how the train is making the storms."

"Cute and fluffy dog? Pink collar?"

Eleazar and I speak at the same time. Our exclamations mix together, and even the magical app can't figure out what we said. Eleazar tries again. "Do you speak Spanish?"

Mariana shakes her head. I can't tell what side of our neighborhood she'd be from. Maybe she has a parent from more than one place, like my dad. I feel a slightly guilty sense of relief that she doesn't speak Spanish. I don't want to be any more left out.

New words pop up on my screen.

"Your dog came through here. As soon as she got into the water, a door appeared and she went right through it. Then the door disappeared before I could get there."

"You should have pet her belly or something," Eleazar says. He looks frustrated. "Don't you know dogs love that? She might have stayed with you. Then she'd still be here now."

Mariana crosses her arms and responds, but I stop paying attention. I think about the poem the train left us and how Mariana knew we were looking for something.

"Are you trying to get through all the train cars too?" I interrupt. "To find the thing you wish for?"

"Sort of. But I'm not going home once I make it." She rolls her eyes and lets out a heavy sigh. "If I ever make it. I'm going to find the Great Conductor, and then I'm going to become his apprentice."

Eleazar and I exchange a glance.

"The Great Conductor takes apprentices?" I ask. "How do you know?"

"My mom told me so many stories about him."

At the word *stories*, I take a step closer to Mariana. I can't help myself.

Her brown eyes light up. For a second I think they flash purple. "Everyone in my family knows the stories of the Great Conductor. He built this train years and years ago. He wears a uniform made out of pure light, and floating instruments follow him around."

My jaw drops. Invincible Girl's cape is pretty cool, but it's not made of pure light.

"Is the *Great Conductor* his real name, or his superhero name?" I ask.

"I don't know. Mom never told me his real name. And when I got to Chicago, I stayed with my great-aunt Lilly until I found the train. She wouldn't tell me his real name either. She said it adds to the mystery and magic if we don't know his name. Like a constellation that hasn't been mapped out yet.

"My mom was his first apprentice," Mariana continues. "The Great Conductor taught her the secrets to all the magic, the way to open every door. She knew where all the hidden bathrooms were, and how to get the train to cook you the very best dinners. She could wish for anything she wanted, and the train would give it to her. She shared its gifts with other kids, traveling all around the world so—"

"Around the world?" Eleazar interrupts. "So this train can go anywhere?"

"Anywhere and everywhere. At least, that's what Mom said."

I think about Barefoot Park and the food. They were sort of like gifts—until they weren't.

And then they really weren't.

"Where's the Great Conductor now?" I ask.

"I don't know," says Mariana. Her lip trembles. I'm glad I can't hear her voice; I know it must be trembling too. "I haven't seen anyone else on the train yet. And Mom said the Great Conductor hated pictures. He only ever took one with her, and she couldn't find it, so I don't know what he looks like. I keep wishing that he'd show up . . . Beverly data waze kit big her."

"Wait, sorry, can you say that louder? I don't think the phone got it." I shake my phone even though I know that won't help. I didn't think magical apps were supposed to make mistakes.

"Every day the waves get bigger," says Mariana. "I want to get out of here."

I gulp. The water looks impossibly deep.

"Have you found any clues?" I ask.

Mariana hesitates and looks us over again before answering. "Kind of. The train is supposed to be filled with riddles, puzzles, and challenges. But the ones Mom told me about made sense.

These clues are weird. All I found when I got here was a map."

She pulls it out of her backpack. The top of the map reads, *Your Treasure Awaits*. It looks dingy and old, like a pirate's map from a movie. Little squiggly lines that look like waves cover the page. A drawing of a skull and crossbones marks a spot in the middle of the map. There are other dots on the page as well, some of them big and some small. It looks like the map of Hawaii we have at school.

"What are all these dots?" I ask. "Is there really stuff out there—in the water?"

"They're islands. You can't see them now, but they appear when you row toward them," she says.

Eleazar hops into the boat. He moves Mariana's bag to make room for himself.

"Why is this so heavy? Did you pack a bunch of rocks or something?"

He shoves Mariana's bag a little too hard, and a bunch of potatoes roll out. Eleazar looks like he's rethinking getting into Mariana's boat.

"Um, potatoes?" I ask.

Mariana crosses her arms defensively. "They have a lot of nutrients."

"There are arepas on this train," Eleazar says. "I don't think you need potatoes."

"Well, I couldn't be sure," Mariana sighs. "Look, when I was little, I wanted to be an astronaut, and I read about growing potatoes in space colonies. You can keep planting new ones with the sprouts, so really they're a perfect food."

"That makes sense," I say. "You got any sweet potatoes?"

"No."

That makes less sense. Sweet potatoes are obviously superior. But right now the thought of *any* food makes my stomach turn. I'm pretty sure that candy monster tried to squirt me with nacho cheese, and I can still smell it.

Mariana looks away. Eleazar picks up her potatoes carefully and puts them back in her bag. I don't want to get into the boat, but it looks like that's our only option, unless we want to swim. (I don't.) The water would get stuck in my ears and make the River of Allergies worse.

But the old, rickety boat doesn't look very safe. This whole train car feels like it belongs in a movie, or out in the suburbs, where people probably have creeks and farms and know how to row boats. It's so different from my neighborhood that I feel far from home. The only boat I've ever been in is a big, slow tour boat at Navy Pier. And it made me sick.

INVINCIBLE GIRL (SOARING ABOVE A LAKE): FLYING IS ALWAYS THE ANSWER.

I sigh and stare at the gray fake-sky above us. If only more Spidey-strings would drop down for us.

Mariana looks doubtful too. "I don't know if my boat is big enough for three people," she says. "Besides, I got here first. The treasure map is meant for me. It's not the clue I was expecting, but . . . my mom made me a map to help me find the train. It led me to Chicago. And then I found this second map. It's the only lead I have."

"Well, we're stuck here with you now. What else are we going to do?" asks Eleazar. He sits in the boat stubbornly.

"I don't know, your dog found her own door when she got into the water. I doubt you two are going to help me any more than she did, so maybe try swimming."

Eleazar's eyebrows furrow angrily, and he swings one of the oars above his head. "Don't talk about Louisa like that! She's the most helpful dog ever."

I'm trying to control the Ms. Suzy app so it can pick everything up, but Eleazar and Mariana start talking to each other so fast that my phone gets confused. I try to mess with it, but it slips from my hand and smacks against the pebbles again, this time leaving a small crack in my screen. *Great.* I can't afford to break my only way to talk to Eleazar. This is why I don't have friends. I don't know what to do when people argue. My head aches and my ears start to buzz. I wish I were a wave. Then the wind could blow me far away from here.

I look up from my cracked phone. Mariana and Eleazar are staring at me.

"What are you doing?" Mariana's words appear on my screen. Eleazar points at my feet. They stopped arguing because I backed into the water without realizing, and now my shoes are all wet. Maybe I'm better at conflict resolution than I think.

"Um, just testing the water. It's too cold to swim, so maybe we should all go in the boat together."

Mariana rolls her eyes. "Fine."

I can't believe that worked. I squish myself into the boat between Mariana and Eleazar, and we take off.

I rub my finger over the crack in my screen—luckily, it's not too bad—while Eleazar rows and Mariana guides him toward the skull and bones on the map. I have a text from Mom asking how things are going.

Good but wet, I say. I'm sure that's true out there in the rain, too.

"Couldn't your mom come with you?" I ask Mariana after I send the text. "To help you find the Great Conductor?"

"She's . . ." She pauses. "She's really far away. But she promised me that I would see the train one day. She knew I'd be able to find it on my own. That's why she made me the map."

She stretches her arms out wide. "And here I am! It makes the long journey feel worth it. I just don't know what's going on with this train car. I can't figure it out."

Eleazar nods. He knows what it's like to have journeyed from a faraway place. But I've never been outside of Chicago. I've never even been to Evanston, and that's only thirty minutes away. Plus, if this is what the suburbs are like, I'm not sure I *want* to leave.

"Look!" Mariana points. "There it is."

There's an island in front of us where there wasn't one before. It's glittering and shiny.

Covered in gold.

"WE'RE RICH!" Eleazar shouts in my ear so loud that my headache doubles in size. I push my fingers against my temples.

Mariana shakes her head. "Being rich won't help us. I don't know what to do. I've already tried on so many crowns. The map says *Your Treasure Awaits*, but I can't find the treasure that's meant for me."

Eleazar doesn't listen to her. He jumps out of the boat and swims to the island.

I grab the oars, push them into the water, and try to pretend like I know what I'm doing. To my surprise, the boat moves forward until it reaches the shore. Mariana and I climb out, and I almost trip over a string of pearls. The sandy shore is covered in sparkling jewels, chests bursting with gold coins, and giant swords that look straight out of a Wonder Woman comic.

Mariana picks up each piece of treasure thoughtfully and looks around, as though she's expecting a door to appear. Eleazar has found pretty much every wearable piece of treasure already. He has a huge gold crown on his head and shiny bronze armor, and he's holding a big staff with a ruby set on top. He pounds the staff into the ground and his lips say, "King!"

Mariana laughs and rushes to put a gold ring on every one of her fingers.

Those two are weird. Just a minute ago they were fighting.

I bend down and pick up a goblet.

Is this what treasure is? I thought it would be something else. My mind floats back to Mom's big orange hoop earrings. The sailboat on Louisa May's collar. The sketchbook in my backpack. *That's* treasure. This is just stuff. I think about the way Mom and I dig through the bins at the thrift store, looking for the most special platters for our Fanksgiving dinners. *The good stuff is always at the bottom.* I plunge my hand into a giant chest and reach around until my fingers find a small gold coin hidden in the corner.

I pull it out and flip the piece of gold over in my hand.

There are a bunch of stars on the coin, connected by thin lines to make a weird shape. Beneath the shape it says *Canis Major*.

"Come look at this!" I say.

Mariana and Eleazar run over to my side. Well, Eleazar tries to run, but his armor is too bulky and his face is covered by the crown, so I'd call it more of a waddle.

As soon as Mariana sees the coin, she claps her hand over her mouth and takes it from me. She runs over to the boat, grabs the oars, and immediately starts pushing off from shore. Eleazar wedges his staff into the bottom of the boat to stop her.

"What are you doing?" I demand. "Were you going to leave us?"

Her cheeks redden. "Sorry," she says. "I got excited. I almost forgot you guys were with me. I usually work alone. But I guess astronauts need other astronauts, right? I'm sorry."

She reaches out to help us into the boat. I take her hand. I know what she means about working alone, but I'm not exactly ready to be her co-astronaut. This train ride is bumpy enough for me—I don't think I could handle outer space.

Mariana pulls the map out again and shows us. Eleazar lifts his crown up so he can get a better look.

"Canis Major is a constellation," Mariana says, tracing the lines on the map with her finger. "I think the skull and crossbones was a distraction. Look at the rest of the islands."

I see it now. They make the same shape as the stars on the coin.

Mariana continues, "I can't believe I didn't see this earlier. See how the constellation is shaped like a dog? This dot right here is the Dog Star. The brightest star in the sky."

"Dog Star? Maybe that'll tell us something about Louisa, too," I say.

In response Eleazar takes all his golden gear off and tosses it onto the shore. Mariana directs us to the Dog Star island. The closer we get, the bigger the waves become. The jar of courage in my stomach lets all the butterflies out, and I feel like I might be sick if we don't get off the rowboat soon. When there are storms over Lake Michigan, the water splashes over the edges of the piers and paths in the city. Out here water just splashes into the boat.

"Can we row faster?" I ask, holding my stomach. I'm not sure if it's the waves, my nerves, or all the food I ate, but if one more wave crashes over my feet, I think I'm going to lose it.

The sky above us grows dark purple clouds, and I have to remind myself that we're still on the train. Mariana looks wary, and I remember what she said. *It isn't supposed to be like this.*

Finally Eleazar points ahead as something huge materializes in front of us, but it's not an island or a star.

It's a ship. It looks like a pirate ship, but it has a bright pink flag. No skull-and-bones in sight. We row over to a ladder hanging down from the ship and climb up to the deck one by one. I let out a deep breath. The waves grow even more, but thankfully, it's a lot more steady up here than it was in the little boat.

Eleazar taps on my shoulder.

He points to a man sleeping on the deck a few feet to our right.

Mariana runs over to him and shakes the man's shoulders urgently, but he sits up lazily.

I think he says, "Yowza!"

He pulls sunglasses out of his jacket pocket, and shakes a grasshopper off the top before he puts them on. Eleazar scrambles backward. I raise my eyebrows at him. I didn't think he was afraid of anything—definitely not bugs.

The grasshopper hops between two panels of wood and disappears belowdecks.

The man doesn't seem to notice that the pet or pest from his pocket ran away. He has light skin, gray hair, and a white beard. He's wearing a dark blue suit with ribbons leaking out the pockets, and instead of shoes he has on roller skates. Underneath his suit jacket he wears a white T-shirt that's printed with two thumbs pointing up at his face, and green words that say, THIS GUY LOVES COOKIES.

He keeps talking, but I don't quite catch all his words.

"Too bright . . . crappy," he says, frowning up at the sky. "Who . . . you . . . long . . . asleep . . ."

I fold my arms across my chest and look down at the man. I think *crappy* is one of the worst-ever words. I usually love words with double letters, but no one likes a double *p*, and I'm not a big fan of words that end in the letter *y*—though I can't seem to avoid them. They always make me ask a question. Sandy (why do you get stuck in my toes?), slippery (why must you make me fall?), cheesy (why so much cheese?), and crappy (really, why are you even a word?).

Mariana says something to the man, but her back is to me, so I can't make out any of her words. Whatever she says seems to confuse him, too.

I take out my phone.

"I don't know what you're talking about," says the man. "My name is Accio Alcatraz. Who are you?"

"It's me, Mariana," she says.

Accio Alcatraz frowns. "I don't know any Mariana."

Mariana pulls a picture of a woman from her pocket.

"What about her? Do you know her? She was the Great Conductor's apprentice."

He leans forward and wrinkles his nose at the photo. "Never seen her in my life."

Mariana takes a step back. Her expression is unsure, confused, and almost hurt. She opens her mouth to speak again, but Accio turns and points at me and Eleazar.

"And who are you?"

"I'm Etta. This is Eleazar."

"What's the name of your pet?" he asks, nodding toward my phone.

"Um, this is just a phone. It doesn't have a name. But this app's called *Ms. Suzy*. I have hearing loss and Eleazar is learning English as a second language, so it helps us understand you."

I think I must be shouting, because the man's eyebrows shoot up into his shaggy gray hair. My cheeks burn a little even though I know I shouldn't be embarrassed.

"Well," he says. "Ms. Suzy spelled my name wrong. Tell your pet it's *A-K-I-O*. Akio."

"She told you it's a phone, not a pet," says Eleazar. "I'm missing my pet, though. Have you seen her? A dog named *Louisa May Alcott*."

"Dogs on the train!" says Akio Alcatraz. There are thick wrinkles on his forehead that move when he speaks. "I sure hope not."

He scratches his cheek and continues, "That reminds me. I've got a few more grievances."

Akio takes off his sunglasses and reaches into his pocket. He pulls out a red leather notebook crawling with ladybugs, and two pencils smaller than my pinky. They remind me of Mom's and Dad's notebooks, and I feel a little pang in my chest. Hopefully Mom is busy painting and won't start worrying about the storms until after I've figured out how to stop them.

A strong gust of wind blows the ladybugs away. Waves crash against the side of the ship, and I almost fall over. Akio stumbles too, and a few bang-snap fireworks fall out of his pocket. They pop and smoke as they hit the ground. This man is a fancy firework if I've ever seen one. An exciting thought enters my mind.

"Are *you* the Great Conductor?"

Akio looks between me and Mariana. "What's all this nonsense about a conductor? There's no conductor here."

My heart sinks. His jacket isn't made out of pure light—it's covered in crumbs. I should have known he wasn't the Great Conductor.

"Yes, there is," says Mariana, crossing her arms. "My mom knew him. She was his apprentice."

"Nonsense. Perhaps there was a conductor, long ago, but he never had an apprentice, and he certainly wasn't great. Your mother told you made-up stories."

"No, she didn't! She promised it was true; she promised before she—"

Mariana stops talking. Her eyes are wide, and I can see her squeezing the Dog Star coin in her hand. She looks horrified.

My toes squirm around uncomfortably in my shoes. I don't know what to say to make her feel better, so I try to change the subject.

"What's in the notebook?"

I peer over Akio's shoulder at the pages in his notebook as he flips through them.

He's written down a list, pages and pages long. It says odd things like:

Grievance #32: Smells like bacon in the exercise room.

Grievance #76: Favorite toilet not flushing.

Grievance #77: Locked inside the bathroom, still not flushing.

Akio turns the pages slowly for me, all the way to the very last page:

Grievance #811: Waves.

Grievance #812: Really big waves.

Grievance #813: Wish for umbrella not working.

He scribbles, **Grievance #814: Dogs apparently allowed now.**

"What do you mean, 'wish not working'?" I ask.

Akio looks at me suspiciously. He writes, **Grievance #815: Humanoid girl named Etta commenting on the nature of my grievances.**

"Asking questions does not make me a grievance! *You'll* be a grievance if you don't answer me. It's rude. So," I say again, "what did you mean 'wish not working'? The food showed up when I was hungry."

And then what happened? he writes.

Eleazar is reading over my shoulder. He puts a hand over his stomach and grimaces.

"The food attacked us," I admit.

Eleazar asks, "So is the train broken, or what?"

I look back at Mariana. She still looks upset. "Hey, you said there was something wrong with the train, didn't you?

You were right! Come look at these grievances."

But instead of coming closer, she takes a few steps back, turns around, and opens a door that must lead belowdecks. She stomps down the stairs and disappears.

I turn back to the notebook, even though a pang of worry THWACKs in my heart. Another wave crashes against the ship. This time it's so big that water spills over the deck.

She's got the right idea, Akio writes. **Let's go inside. It's far too bright out here.**

Even if he's not the Great Conductor, he might be able to help us. Eleazar runs down belowdecks immediately.

"We're looking for our treasure so we can get to the next train car," I say. "And you don't have to write everything. You can just talk into my phone."

Akio writes, **I will not talk to your pet.**

"Okay, talk your regular way, then," I say. The microphone will catch his words anyway.

"I don't have any treasure down belowdecks," Akio says. "But I have lots of tea."

CHAPTER 13

AKIO WAS WRONG. He has *lots* of treasure. None of it is gold, but it all looks like it's probably important to him. After he clomped down the stairs on his roller skates, he brought us into the main part of the ship. I'm pretty sure he lives here.

There are three stoves and at least eight different beautifully painted teapots. Brightly covered tapestries hang on the walls and over the windows, giving the space a cozy glow. An old record player at least the size of Louisa May hangs out in the corner, surrounded by posters of bands I don't know. There's also a trampoline and a pinball machine.

And there are cookies everywhere. So many cookies.

"Do you want a cookie?" Akio asks.

"Definitely not. I mean, thank you. But no." My stomach hurts bad enough as it is.

Mariana sits down at a table in the middle of the room and crosses her arms. She was expecting treasure, and instead she got a man on roller skates who said her mom made everything up. I feel bad, but I don't know what to say. When she found the clue about the Dog Star, she got back onto the boat so fast and tried to leave without us. I bet she wishes we hadn't shown up. But there's nowhere else for us to go now, so I join her at the table. Eleazar plops down next to me.

Akio sets yellow cups in front of us and pours tea from a pot shaped like a cat, but he still looks suspicious.

Beside me Eleazar frowns. He pulls my phone close to his mouth and talks into it. I read his words, translated from Spanish. "Are you sure we should be stopping to have tea?"

His fingers tap impatiently on the table while he waits for me to respond. He doesn't want to waste any more time—we need to get Louisa.

"We need them to find the door to the next train car," I say. And the tea smells like ginger. It might help me feel less like I'm about to throw up—but I don't say that out loud.

Eleazar chews his lip. I reach out my hand to reassure him that I'm serious about finding Louisa, but he puts on a fake smile and raises his teacup. He tries to clink cups with Mariana, but she only frowns at him. The ship rocks with the waves, and two of the teapots roll into each other and crack into pieces. Akio sweeps them into a giant pile of broken glass in the corner. His lips move in fast, small movements, like he's grumbling to himself.

He looks up at us. "How did you find the train anyway?" he asks, speaking loudly enough for my microphone.

"I followed my mom's map to Chicago," Mariana says. She looks proud. "Then I tracked the storm and the fireworks."

"You think that the storms started with the fireworks explosion from the engine?" I ask. "That's what we think, but we weren't sure."

"My mom said that the train affects everyone around it,"

Mariana says. "She even told me something about blue fireworks changing the weather. . . . She wasn't talking about storms, though. But I still figured it out."

"Did she say anything about how to stop them?" I ask eagerly. "We think the storms are doing weird things like making people sad, and making people not be able to write their comics, and, uh . . ." I pause and hope Mariana doesn't know that *people* means me.

"Storms . . ." Akio scribbles something else in his book of grievances. "That explains it. I was sleeping peacefully until two weeks ago, when the train started running again after all these years and the waves came."

"Have you been here for years?" Eleazar spills his tea.

"Wait. Akio Alcatraz . . . ," I say. "Isn't Alcatraz—"

"The inescapable prison." Akio nods.

Oh no. "Is that what this train is?" I ask.

"No," says Akio, tapping his forehead. "It's what this is."

He's trapped inside his own mind. I think I know that feeling. The boat rocks, and Akio's chair tips all the way over. I wonder if he'll be mad if I throw up in one of his teapots.

"How long has it been since the train ran?" He must be so lonely here.

"It's been a number of years."

"What does that mean? Two years or fifty years?" Eleazar demands.

"Yes, those are both numbers," Akio says from the floor. I glare at him. "Drink your tea," he says.

I do. The spicy ginger settles my stomach.

"All I know is that something really terrible must have happened to wake this beast. I felt it in the air and in my—" He clutches at his heart, and his words stop popping up on my screen.

"Did you say *beast*?" I ask.

Akio looks at me like he can't believe I would ask such a silly question. "Of course. The train is a beast, like any other creature."

"*Creature?* Are you saying this thing is alive?"

"It runs, doesn't it? It has direction. What's the difference between that and life?"

Eleazar peeks at the translation, then looks at me and

shrugs. I don't know either. Water leaks in through the boards above us. I look at Akio in alarm, but he places his chair back upright and sips his tea like nothing's wrong.

"What else do you know about the train?" Mariana asks. Her face is set, like she's challenging Akio to say something else about her mom's stories.

"Me? I don't know anything. I've been here between two and fifty years. And there were never any waves or storms until a few weeks ago. I'm not the one messing things up. Are you?"

"No," I protest. "We were still at home a few weeks ago. And what about—"

Akio interrupts me. "I can't remember the rest."

"Do you at least know where we can find our treasures?" Eleazar asks.

Akio narrows his eyes. "You're all looking for something?"

We nod. I realize we all have that in common. Mariana's looking for the Great Conductor, Eleazar's looking for Louisa May Alcott, and I . . . I know I'm here to help Eleazar and Mom, but I feel like I'm looking for something else, too. I must be, or the train wouldn't have made a ticket with my name on it.

What's my wish? I don't know exactly. There are still so many blank pages in my sketchbook. The water continues leaking through the ceiling until it fills the room up to my ankles. Akio sips his tea.

"It kind of seems like the storms are getting worse," I say as politely as I can.

The boat rocks so far to the side that all the furniture crashes into one of the walls—and us along with it. I hold my phone close to my chest so it doesn't get damaged.

"What's that you said?" Akio asks calmly. His teacup is still upright in his hand.

"I said the storms are getting worse! We need to get out of here and find our treasure!"

"I can't help with treasure," Akio says. "But there's a door in my closet."

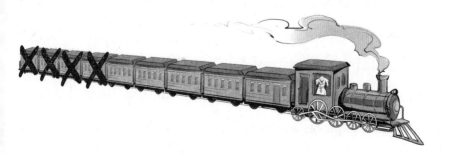

CHAPTER 14

IT'S SNOWING in the next train car: light, soft flakes that must be made of something more than ice crystals. These are little bits of lace, strands of angel hair, warm reminders of sunlight and spring. Yes, warm. *These snowflakes are warm.* One falls on the tip of my nose; I stay very still and try to look at it but keep crossing my eyes. I can feel it there, though, as soft as a kiss from Dad.

Little bursts of warmth fall into my hair and onto my arms, like someone took a hammer to the sun and cracked it, and now all the pieces are in this magical train car, falling to the floor. I think about what Eleazar said when we were walking to my house—how he missed the warm rain in Colombia and would rather have snow. He got his wish. And so did I.

But a million times better. Especially compared to the splashing water in the last train car. I can't believe Akio had a door in his closet that whole time and didn't tell us. I don't understand why it appeared, since we didn't find any treasure, but I'm glad to be off that boat.

Small white crystals land on the piece of hair in front of Eleazar's face. He shakes them onto the floor.

The floor! I clap my hands over my mouth. Happy tears dance in my eyes. The floor is covered in *books*, tall piles and short piles and piles half-hidden by the snow. I spin in a circle twice to soak it all in. We're standing in a world of words where books spread over the floor like dandelions growing in a park. This train car is bigger than the Harold Washington Library, bigger than *any* library. It's better than good. It's the best thing I've ever seen.

Akio holds up a striped book that's as thick as a dictionary. "I forgot about this book. It's an epic tale of epic proportions.

Very exciting. Can't put it down. Just a few more years, and I think I'll be finished with it."

Maybe instead of writer's block, like what's keeping me from making comics, he has reader's block. Invincible Girl wouldn't spend years reading books as thick as her head.

Akio picks up his book, brings it to his nose, and begins reading. Within three seconds he has fallen over. Eleazar rushes forward and looks him over carefully.

"He's asleep."

"What? Are you serious?"

Eleazar shrugs. "My grandma could fall asleep anywhere too."

Mariana watches Akio cautiously. I can tell she's still upset that he was talking about her mom.

"Are you okay?" I ask her.

"Whose wish is this?" she demands. "I didn't wish for books."

"Um, I think it's mine," I say a little guiltily. "I was thinking about my sketchbook."

I don't tell them I was thinking about blank pages. The train knew what I wanted—books filled with words and stories.

"What were you wishing for?" Eleazar asks Mariana.

"Space," she says, as though that were the most obvious thing in the world. "I told you I want to be an astronaut."

"I thought you wanted to be the Great Conductor's apprentice."

She looks flustered. "Well, they're kind of the same. I want to be in charge of whatever machine takes you to sights unseen."

Eleazar's lips repeat *sights unseen*. He raises an eyebrow at me.

"I think you just want to be in charge," he says.

Mariana turns her back to him and covers her face with the book closest to her.

Eleazar grimaces and pushes the hair out of his face. He gestures to the books. Seems like there's nothing we can do to help Mariana but read. I'm not mad about it, though.

"Guess we should start reading," I say. "The clue to find the door must be in these books."

I tiptoe around the endless library, careful not to knock anything over. The floor is covered in books of every size, with loopy words printed across the covers. My head clouds, and all the books blur together. I try to blink the feeling away. There are more stories here than I could ever write.

Maybe there's more than a clue to help us find the door. There might be something that would explain what's wrong with the train's magic and what the storm is doing to our families. I look over the never-ending stacks. It'll be nearly impossible to pick out a book about the train with so many here, but if there's any challenge I'm up for, it's a *book* challenge. I pick up a pile of books. The smallest one has a picture of four girls on the cover. I gasp. It's *Little Women*.

"Look! It's another copy of *Mu—*"

I realize partway through the word that I have no idea how to pronounce Eleazar's book *Mujercitas*, so I'm pretty sure I end up making a sound like a cow and then stop. The tops of my ears burn.

I wish for invisibility. I wish for it *hard*.

Eleazar ignores my embarrassing noise. He leans in close to my phone and says something into it.

"'She is too fond of books, and it has turned her brain.'"

"Huh? Turned my brain into what?"

"My grandma told me Louisa May Alcott said that. I think it's a compliment."

"Your *dog* said that?" I say.

Eleazar rolls his eyes, then looks away, embarrassed.

I really do know what he meant. And he has a point. I hold the pile of books tight to my chest and hope he can't hear the good kind of THWACKs coming from my heart.

He keeps talking.

"I know Louisa May Alcott only writes books for girls. But this was my grandma's favorite. She gave me this book when I left Colombia."

My chest THWACKs again, this time angrily. All the books fall out of my arms.

"There's no such thing as books for girls and boys! There's only books, and words, and you can't just say you don't like half of them! It's like saying you only like half the alphabet, but you couldn't even spell your name if you only had *A* through *M*!"

My nostrils flare—like I'm wearing a new sign, different from the one I got when we were at my house yesterday: HERE

IS A GIRL WHO HAD A CHANCE TO BE COOL AND DECIDED
SHE'D REALLY RATHER NOT.

Eleazar points at my flared nostrils. "You look like my
grandma when she's mad. She always said the same thing."
His words stop showing up on my app for a second while he
pauses. "I did like it. I like Beth. And Laurie. My grandma liked
Laurie. She knew a lot about stories. I used to draw pictures in
all her books."

I let out a big relieved breath and put *Little Women* in my
backpack to read as soon as all of this is over.

Eleazar picks a tall, thin book out of a small pile almost
entirely covered in snow.

The title is printed in the same font as some of my schoolbooks. It's written in Spanish.

El Gran Incendio de Chicago

I retype it into the translator.

The Great Chicago Fire

THWACK-THWACK.

That doesn't sound too good.

Eleazar doesn't look excited to find this book either. He

tosses it aside. "Why would I want a book about Chicago? I don't even like—"

The translator stops filling in his words again. He looks uncomfortable.

"Were there any trains involved in the fire?" I ask. "It could be useful, maybe. A book about trains might help us figure out what's wrong with this one. Translating would take up a lot of my phone battery, but . . . I could read it if you want."

"It's okay. I'll read it." He sighs and picks up the book again. "If it's boring, I'll find another one. Do you think there are clues inside?"

"Probably. Keep your eye out for more weird capital letters."

I grab a few more books. There's one filled with kale recipes that Mom would love. When I toss it aside, a gold pen falls out from between the pages and lands in the snow.

That's weird. I pick the pen up. It feels heavy, like it's filled with something more than ink. My fingers itch to use it. But I won't find any clues or facts about the train writing my own words. I look around at the others. Mariana has fallen asleep behind her book, and Eleazar looks like he's about to doze off too.

Maybe I could write a little.

I pull my sketchbook out of my backpack and use the pen to make a tiny scribble in the corner of a blank page. It's not just the pen that's gold—it's the ink, too. It looks like melted metal, and it sits on top of the page instead of sinking into the paper. I touch the gold ink with my hand, but it doesn't budge. *Smudge-proof liquid gold.* It's magical.

My heart THWACKs.

This was made for me.

A thought from two days ago enters my mind: *C'mon, Etta, surely you don't believe everything that happens in books.*

But I do. Now I'm holding the proof in my hands. I sink to the floor. My fingers shake; my eyes fill. I feel strange and special, like I do on my birthday when everybody watches me blow out candles. Only now, my wish is already sitting on my lap.

The train is helping me write the Invincible Girl story I've always wanted to tell. I can only imagine what kind of masterpiece Mom would paint if she were here too.

I place the tip of the pen back onto the paper and start working on the script for my Invincible Girl comic.

INVINCIBLE GIRL (FLYING THROUGH THE SKY): I'M COMING FOR YOU, PETRA FIDE, AND I'M NOT SCARED AT ALL!

CHAPTER 15

A SPEEDING TRAIN FLIES THROUGH A DARK CITY. DR. PETRA FIDE IS AT THE HELM, HER BULKY LASER BLASTERS AT HER SIDE. THE TRAIN IS FILLED WITH PEOPLE IN LAB COATS. ROPES TIE THEIR HANDS AND FEET.

DR. PETRA FIDE (CACKLING): ONCE I GET THEM TO MY LAB, I'LL MAKE THE GREATEST WEAPON THE WORLD HAS EVER SEEN. WITH IT BY MY SIDE, ALL THE POWER—

MAN: WE'LL NEVER HELP YOU BUILD THAT CREATURE. AND WITHOUT OUR HELP, IT'LL NEVER BREATHE A SINGLE FLAME—

DR. PETRA FIDE (AIMING HER LASER AT THE MAN):

I DO WANT YOUR HELP, SO I'LL GIVE YOU ONE MORE CHANCE TO LIVE. ANSWER THIS: WHAT HAS TWO WINGS, GREEN EYES, PLAYS WITH FIRE, AND NEVER DIES?

MAN (SHAKING HIS HEAD): I WON'T HELP WITH THAT.

DR. PETRA FIDE FIRES. A PURPLE LASER HITS THE MAN SQUARE IN THE CHEST. HIS BODY FREEZES IN PLACE. ONLY HIS EYES MOVE BACK AND FORTH. A WOMAN AT THE END OF THE TRAIN CAR SOBS.

WOMAN: IS THERE NO ONE LEFT TO HELP US?

INVINCIBLE GIRL: I WILL.

DR. PETRA FIDE: INVINCIBLE GIRL, IT'S YOU, ISN'T IT?

WOMAN: INVINCIBLE GIRL, BE CAREFUL! THE CREATURE FIDE'S MAKING IS TOO DANGEROUS . . . WINGS MADE OF METAL AND FIRE AT ITS CORE. SAVE US, PLEASE!

INVINCIBLE GIRL: HAND OVER THESE PEOPLE, AND THE OTHER THING YOU TOOK FROM ME.

DR. PETRA FIDE (CACKLING): AND WHAT WOULD THAT BE? COULD IT BE THAT I GOT AWAY WITH ONE OF YOUR PRECIOUS BOOKS? YOU THOUGHT YOU'D DEFEATED ME, BUT YOU NEVER HAVE.

INVINCIBLE GIRL: I'LL GET IT BACK FROM YOU. AND YOU'LL NEVER BE ABLE TO BUILD WHATEVER WEAPON YOU'RE PLANNING.

DR. PETRA FIDE: WHY DOES IT EVEN MATTER TO YOU? IT'S JUST A BOOK, AFTER ALL.

INVINCIBLE GIRL: PERHAPS I AM TOO FOND OF BOOKS. PERHAPS THEY'VE TURNED MY BRAIN. BUT THE FACT REMAINS: YOUR TIME'S UP.

INVINCIBLE GIRL RAISES HER FISTS.

DR. PETRA FIDE: IF YOU WANT IT BACK, YOU'LL HAVE TO ANSWER MY RIDDLE FIRST.

INVINCIBLE GIRL: I'D EXPECT NOTHING LESS FROM YOU.

DR. PETRA FIDE: WHAT TWISTS ALL YOUR FOOLISH DREAMS, TANGLES HOPES, BUT IS FUN FOR ME?

My fingers tingle with excitement at the thought of Invincible Girl defeating her archnemesis, but I can't seem to write any more. Snow falls around me, warm and sweet. The snowflakes weave together like a spider's web, growing thicker and heavier until it feels like I'm lying under a big, white blanket. My eyelids feel so heavy; I can barely keep them open. My magic pen slips out from between my fingers.

I let the warmth of the train car swallow me up, and I fall asleep on a bed of books.

The world is spinning.

Where am I?

Where am I?

Snow falls onto my eyelashes. I'm still on the train. Magic caramel and hot dogs aren't mixing together so well in my stomach. The blanket of snow feels almost like it's made of ice or rock. It grows heavy and pushes against me, harder and harder until suddenly I feel like I can't breathe.

I can't breathe.

Dizziness overwhelms me, but all my limbs are frozen. The ringing in my ears is louder than ever. Snow catches on my eyelids, making the room blurry, and I can't tell if my body is shaking or the whole train car is rattling. I need to find something solid to focus on. But I can't move.

I lie frozen in the spinning world for more minutes than I

can count. Finally I use all my strength to force my head to the side. There's a small blue book on the ground next to me. I focus on one of its corners while everything behind it spins. I take deep, gasping breaths, and slowly the whole book comes into focus, and then the other books around it, and then the snow stops swirling and my limbs become my own again.

I sit up and push the heavy snowflakes off me. I look at my phone. It's after two o'clock—I slept for *hours*. My battery is only at 30 percent, and I have about a hundred texts from Mom. She says the storms outside are getting worse. I don't tell her that the storms inside are too. I text back, Everything's good. Had lunch with Eleazar. That part's true, even though I don't say what we had for lunch or that we ate on the train. Mom probably thinks I'm at Eleazar's house. Going to keep looking for Louisa, be home soon. I hit send. The ringing in my ears doesn't go away. I don't know for sure that I'll be home soon.

Eleazar and Akio are still asleep, but Mariana's sitting up in the corner with the gold pen and a book—*my book*.

"What are you doing?" I demand.

She looks up at me and smiles. She has no idea I just had a

vertigo attack on the floor. I open the Ms. Suzy app with shaky fingers.

"This is so cool," she says, holding up my pen. "What did you wish for to get this?"

"I don't know. . . . I guess . . . I don't like blank pages."

"Well, I filled some in for you!"

I feel like I'm going to throw up again. I can't believe she took my sketchbook, and then *wrote in it*? All without asking. She probably read the stuff that's in there too. I want to hide under a pile of books and never come out. But first I want my sketchbook back.

"Can I have it back? I don't like people reading my work." I know I sound mean, but I'm focusing too much on not throwing up to pretend I'm not upset. I'm pretty sure the Great Conductor won't want an apprentice who takes stuff from the passengers.

Mariana gives back the book and pen. She added her own gold words to my script.

INVINCIBLE GIRL: I'M NOT HERE TO SOLVE YOUR RIDDLES, FIDE. YOU'RE SMALL POTATOES COMPARED TO ME! STOP WASTING MY TIME.

PETRA FIDE: I BET YOU'RE NOT ANSWERING BECAUSE YOU DON'T KNOW THE ANSWER!

INVINCIBLE GIRL: NO, THAT'S DEFINITELY NOT IT. I TOTALLY KNOW THE ANSWER.

PETRA FIDE: I KNOW THE ANSWER TOO.

INVINCIBLE GIRL: TO WHAT?

PETRA FIDE: YOUR WEAKNESS. THAT'S WHY I TURNED THESE BLASTERS INTO FLAMETHROWERS!

INVINCIBLE GIRL: NOT FIRE! NOOOOOOOOO!

The last line ends with a description of Invincible Girl on the ground, terrified and hurt. I round on Mariana.

"What did you do?! Fire can't hurt Invincible Girl."

"I thought it was fun. It's not exciting if she beats the villain easily."

"You don't understand," I say, fighting back tears. The snowflakes falling on my face feel like tiny, piercing darts. "Invincible Girl doesn't have a weakness. That's why they call her invincible."

"Why are you getting so upset? It's just a story."

"It's not just a story to me!"

I flip the pen over and scrub the gold eraser against the paper so hard, the paper rips. But it's no use. The magical ink doesn't budge.

Mariana recoils. Then she throws her hands over her head in the air like she's exasperated with me. She retreats back to her corner to get another book. The snowflakes coming down now are hard pebbles of ice.

Eleazar sits up and looks at the two of us.

"You okay?" he says. "What happened?"

I don't want to tell him about the vertigo or the story. Not yet. It'll just make him feel sorry for me. Maybe he'll even wish I hadn't come along.

I just say, "I'm okay."

He doesn't look like he believes me, but he doesn't say anything more either.

"I haven't found any clues yet," he says. "I'll keep looking."

He circles the train car, staring at the titles on all the book covers. I should start searching the other books too. But I can't leave Invincible Girl's story like this.

I pick up the gold pen and open to the last panel I was

working on. But as soon as the magical tip touches the page, I yawn. My eyelids feel heavy again. Then a push on my shoulder makes me force my eyes open.

Eleazar stands over me. "Etta, you were falling asleep again. What's going on?"

I look over at Mariana, who's asleep with a book open in her lap. Akio hasn't moved.

We're stuck in the middle of our stories. Akio said that he's been reading for *years* and still hasn't finished his book. He takes too many naps, but maybe it's not just because he's old. Maybe that's the train's magic. The soft snow is a magical lullaby, luring us to sleep. And the train will keep us here, trapped in a loop of sleeping and writing and reading and sleeping until well past my curfew.

We have to find a way to move on. Past the middle and the maybe. "I don't know exactly what's happening," I say. "The train gave us books; it must want us to read them. But we keep falling asleep in the middle of the stories. There has to be a clue here. But we're missing it."

Eleazar nods. "It's a trick or something."

"Can I see the first book you were reading?"

He finds it and hands it to me.

I flip through the pages until I get to the very last one. Only, it's not actually the last page—I can't read all the words in Spanish, but it looks like the story ends in the middle of a sentence. I open a few more books and flip through the pages. They're the same. If a book and all its pages are pieces of a puzzle, fit together to make a story, then all these books are missing the last piece.

Eleazar looks over my shoulder. He seems to come to the same realization I do.

"All the books are missing the end," he says. "I bet we can't find the door until we get to the end of the stories. But how do we do that?"

I look at the pen in my hand. I'm the writer of my story—if I want to get through this train car, I just have to finish it.

"We finish the stories ourselves," I say.

"Can I see your copy of *Little Women?*" he says. "I know how that ends."

I hand it to him, then open my own sketchbook. I skip

to the very last page and start to write, *THE END.* I hesitate over the letters and scratch them out before I finish. This can't be the end. It's the end of this train car because we need to go on, but I haven't finished my story yet. I'm not over the wall. Invincible Girl *has* to win. I try to write another line, taking back the weakness Mariana gave to Invincible Girl, but I get sleepy and dizzy again. This is the only thing I can think of to try. But once I do it, it can't be erased.

Invincible Girl will lose.

I finish the story anyway. *THE END.*

I hand Eleazar the magical pen, and he scribbles something on the last page of *Little Women.* A door, painted as white as a snowflake, appears on top of a pile of books. Our way forward. But there's a rock in the pit of my stomach. I'm so frustrated. With Mariana and myself. Invincible Girl was supposed to beat Fide and figure out the storms. If Invincible Girl can be defeated . . . if I can't even make my hero beat a supervillain in a make-believe story, what hope is there for me here?

The ringing in my ears is like a choir of high-pitched bees. Mariana yawns and sits up slowly. She stretches as small snow pebbles fall onto her head. It feels a little cooler than it did before.

I look down at my phone. I'm using up so much battery with the Ms. Suzy app. And now that Mom seems to be texting me every few minutes, my battery is draining even faster. I ignore her latest check-in and open the translator.

"What happened?" Mariana asks. I don't make eye contact with her.

"You fell asleep again."

"We found the door," Eleazar says.

Mariana's head turns, and she stares at the door in amazement. "Awesome! Let's get out of here. Ouch!"

Bits of snow fall onto my head and my nose. They're not gentle flakes anymore. It feels like someone dumped a bunch of little rocks onto my head, which is not something anyone I know would do.

Akio wakes up too. He holds his book of grievances over his head and glares at us.

"What did you all do? You kids, I swear, the worst cooks I've ever seen. Can't a man enjoy his nap in peace? This train will take any fuel it can get, doesn't know what's good for it, doesn't know a thing—"

"What do you mean, fuel?" I say, taking cover under my backpack.

The ticket in my pocket says *Pays with fuel.* But I don't have any fuel. I'm not sure what Akio's talking about.

Akio Alcatraz points at us. "The train eats what's inside you, and what's inside you tastes *bad.*"

I almost stick out my tongue to see if the snow actually tastes bad, but the hail is getting bigger and my stomach turns, reminding me of what happened in the train car with all the food.

There's no time to figure out what Akio is saying. We have to get out of here.

Eleazar swats big pieces of hail away with a giant book.

Mariana covers her head with her arms and rushes toward the door.

I put my sketchbook and magic pen into my backpack before standing, but Akio doesn't move.

"I was happy here," he says. His face is twisted and angry.

"Now the train's broken. It's the wrong kind of hungry and has the wrong kind of cooks feeding it."

"I don't know why you keep calling us cooks," I say. "But I know you can't stay here."

I don't know how to get him back to his ship either. I guess he's stuck with us.

Eleazar reaches out a hand and pulls Akio up. He wobbles on his skates as we head for the door.

If we figure out what Akio's trying to say about cooks, it might help us learn how the train works. Akio seems to know more about the train than he's telling us. Either way, I've got a grievance to add to his list.

Grievance #816: Magical libraries should be 100 percent safe.

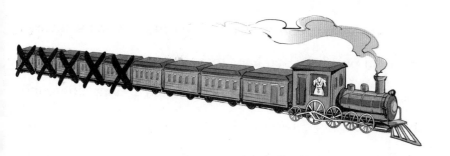

CHAPTER
16

THE NEXT TRAIN car is an actual room, with four walls and a ceiling. Thankfully, there's no hail here, but it looks more like a giant gym than a regular train car. The floors are covered in extra-shiny wood, and the walls are as white as a blank page in my sketchbook.

There are no doors or windows set into the walls. Instead dozens of punching bags hang from the ceiling—they look like big, colorful blobs, like someone splattered paint all around the train car.

The four of us look at one another.

"Who wished for this?" Akio asks. "There's something not right here."

"There's something not right *everywhere*," I say. I toss my backpack against the wall in frustration, but I immediately regret it. I'm not sure that I'm a backpack-tossing kind of person.

Right above the place where my backpack hit, the word *BAM!* appears on the wall in bold yellow letters, surrounded by a spiky red oval.

I look around at the paper-colored walls again and run my hand over the thick, plastic-feeling material covering one of the punching bags. I think I'm standing inside a real live comic.

INVINCIBLE GIRL (STARING AT A GIRL WHO LOOKS AN AWFUL LOT LIKE ETTA JOHNSON): HUH? WHAT ARE YOU DOING HERE?

A feeling fills my heart, big and painful and pounding in my ears. *I'm not supposed to be here.* The ending of my comic is ruined. I don't deserve to be standing inside one.

I look at Eleazar, but he's busy walking around the zigzag patterns of hanging punching bags.

I walk over to the word *BAM!* splayed across the wall.

There are two blue boxing gloves on the ground next to the spot where my bag landed.

I pull them onto my hands.

There's a lumpy yellow punching bag a few feet from my right hand. I look around to make sure no one's watching me—I don't want anyone else to see that spending long hours writing stories hasn't made my arm muscles any bigger—before throwing a soft punch at the bag. As my fist collides with the shiny fabric, the word *WHAM!* appears on the wall, painted out like a comic book exclamation. The punching bag sways back and forth. I draw a sharp breath in.

My punch was a lot harder than I thought it'd be.

My eyebrows scrunch together. I squeeze the inside of the gloves as hard as I can. The punch felt like a bolt of lightning spreading through the muscles in my arm. It felt *good*. The spark of lightning moves from my arm to my chest before filling my stomach with an angry storm that thunders with every bad thing that's happened.

I understand what I wished for now, the thing I wanted

from the train. *A perfect comic*. The gold pen was going to get me there. I wanted to show off my story to Mom and maybe even Eleazar and Mariana, but I wanted to do it on my own terms. Not have Mariana take my book while I was asleep. I wanted to be someone brave, but maybe the train understands my true self. I tried to write my story, and Invincible Girl ended up being as cowardly as I am. Now the train's taunting me with this comic-colored car. My fist crunches into the punching bag again. I feel like my jar of courage got smashed to smithereens.

POW!

The bag splits open like a piñata, and a pile of random pieces of metal, gears, wires, and glass falls to the floor.

Whoa. I'm definitely not this strong.

Unless . . . a blizzard of thoughts blows around in my mind. I've always wished for superpowers, haven't I?

Maybe the train is broken so some of our wishes aren't working, like Akio said, but that doesn't mean it's not paying attention to us. Punching bags and superpowers and comic book words on the walls. I think I made this train car. Maybe it's a chance to rewrite my comic. My chance to be invincible.

I walk to the back wall and crouch down with my right leg braced in front of my left like a sprinter waiting for their race to start.

My feet take off, but my fists fly faster. I run through the center of the train car, hitting each bag I pass as hard as any superhero could. Gears and wires spill onto the floor as the bags burst open.

I punch one for days that are too quiet.

One for days that are too loud. For the thank-you promise I don't know how to keep. For seventeen days of storms with no sun. Mean bus drivers. Missing dogs.

I dig my heels into the floor, slide, and screech to a halt right in front of a huge blue bag. I lift my arm for another blow and spot Eleazar and Mariana out of the side of my eye. Eleazar has on red boxing gloves, and Mariana has yellow ones. Both of them are breathing hard.

They're fighting too. Eleazar's fist makes contact with a punching bag and sends it flying halfway across the room.

SMACK! THUMP! KERSPLAT!

My fist penetrates all the way through the big, blue bag. More scraps of metal fly across the room.

I turn around, gasping for air.

We have superstrength. Maybe we're not such bad cooks after all.

Eleazar looks at me. He's still never admitted that he's scared. But he must be angry. We've been on the train all this time, and we're still so far away from Louisa.

Mariana has rage in her cheeks, colored red. She hasn't found what she's looking for either.

Akio skates through all the mess with his hands behind his back, shaking his head at us.

I pull off my boxing gloves, grab my backpack, and throw it back onto my shoulders. I can't let go of my books. Even if Invincible Girl's story is over, mine might not be. There's a big part waiting for us at the end—Louisa May Alcott. And the Great Conductor might know how to erase magic gold ink.

I open my app. There's only a quarter of my battery left. "If we're this strong," I call out, "let's just punch our way through all the train cars."

Eleazar smiles and throws a few more air punches. "We wouldn't have to find any more clues if we do that," he agrees.

Mariana shakes her head. "We won't be this strong if we leave."

"Why not?" I ask.

"My mom said that everything you find here, you're supposed to leave behind when you're ready."

Eleazar crosses his arms awkwardly, trying to tuck his boxing gloves beneath his elbows. "What if we're not ready to leave this behind?"

"I wasn't ready to leave my boat behind." Akio's mouth scrunches up grumpily as he skates over to speak into my phone.

I remember how sleepy and warm I felt when the snow was falling. And how quickly that magical feeling left when we found the door and it started hailing.

"Mariana's right," I say, even though I don't want to admit it. "The magic is different in every train car. I bet we won't have any of this strength when we leave."

Eleazar makes an annoyed face and tries to do the sign I taught him for *awful* with his gloves still on.

"The things my mom said are making less and less sense," says Mariana, kicking at a gear on the ground. "The train sounded so great when I was a kid, but now I don't know. Why should we have to leave stuff behind?"

She punches one of the last bags, and it flies all the way across the train car, just barely missing Akio's head.

Mariana takes a step back. She looks surprised by her own strength.

Akio glides in a circle around us. His skates leave deep purple grooves in the floor.

"Stop this! Punching! Violence! You're going to make everything worse. Whatever you put into the oven is going to burn unless you stop."

"Why?" challenges Mariana. "We're finally strong. Might as well fight before we have to give it all up."

There are only two punching bags still swinging from the ceiling. Eleazar hits one of them, sending more gears and pieces of metal flying across the train car.

"Maybe the boxing gloves were the clues for this train car," Eleazar says. "And the solution is to hit everything."

If that's the way through, then this train is getting even more messed up. And it feels so good to let everything out.

I tried to share my story with the train, but it took it and twisted it with hail and fire blasters. I don't want to be weak anymore. I don't want to get stuck here.

I just want to fight.

Superstrength fills my muscles with electricity. Fear THWACKs in my chest.

Akio wags his finger at us. "You cook with the wrong ingredients. You cook with—"

BAM! I punch the last bag with a gloveless fist.

It explodes in a thick cloud of purple smoke and dust and flying gears.

I cover my mouth with my sleeve and blink the dust out of my eyes.

The dust settles and the gears fall to the ground. A door appears at the far end of the room. But in front of it, a figure emerges from the purple cloud. It's a woman in a white lab coat. She has blue hair and light skin. Purple-tinted goggles cover half her face.

And there are two giant blasters at her side.

It's Petra Fide.

CHAPTER 17

PETRA FIDE TAPS the side of her goggles as she surveys the destroyed punching bags. My heart pounds with the THWACK-THWACK of terror and awe mixed together. *How is she here?*

"Well, well, well, look at the damage you've done. I see you came ready for a fight."

Fide's words appear on my phone screen. My arms are sore from all the punching. I'm not sure I feel strong anymore.

I turn to Eleazar, trying to see if there's a sentence in his eyes, a secret we could share that would get us out of here, but all I see in Eleazar is fear. I gave him my Fide comic before we even got on the train. He knows I created her, and now she's found a way out of the pages—to stand in front of us, tall and menacing.

Eleazar shuffles over to my side. Mariana and Akio move closer too—all four of us stand in a huddle near the back of the train car, facing Petra Fide.

She steps toward us. I stumble backward, half tripping over one of the gears on the floor. The ringing in my ears screeches like a siren. *Danger. Danger.* But sirens usually mean that help is on the way. And I don't think anyone is coming to save us.

A wave of dizziness rushes over me. My doctor would tell me now is the time to *de-stress*. But I don't think my doctor has ever faced a supervillain.

Fide smiles. "Or maybe you're not so ready to fight. You'd better choose: Are you going to stay or run?"

She waves her blasters at another door that's just appeared behind us. The train is giving us a way out. And I want to take it. Maybe we *have* gone far enough, and there's nothing ahead of us but the pulsing, painful ringing in my ears.

I could go back, get off the train, and buy a new sketch-book. Start over with a new story and a new friend.

No. I clutch the straps of my backpack and stand still at Eleazar's side. I may not get to write the perfect Invincible Girl comic, but I can still keep my promise.

I asked for a fight, and I got one.

"Staying?" says Fide. "Excellent. I'll just make sure you aren't tempted to leave."

She aims her blasters at the new door behind us and zaps it with a purple laser. The handle melts, and more purple smoke rises into the air.

The smell of licorice and charcoal reaches my nose. It burns the inside of my nostrils and throat when I breathe it in. I start coughing.

Petra Fide throws back her head and laughs. Her horrible smile takes up the bottom half of her face, and the rest of her is masked behind huge comic-style glasses. Just the way I drew her. Another feeling—guilt as sharp as the glass that burst out of the punching bags—joins the fear currently gluing me to the floor. It's my fault that Fide's here.

"Do you feel that? I call it The Fear. Capital *T*, capital *F*," she says with a wink. "That's it, let it grow. With my new weapon, I'll be able to spread The Fear far and wide. No one will be able to fight it. Once they all lose hope, the world will fall under my control, one person, one family, one city at a time. Which of your families will fall first, I wonder? Which of you is most afraid?"

My heart THWACKs. I glance at Eleazar. *One family, one city?* Whatever weapon Fide's talking about . . . she's going to use it to hurt the world outside the train too. It doesn't make any sense. She's not the one who started all this. The storms are coming from the train, not Fide. She's *my* creation.

But she seems real. And the blaster definitely works. I used Fide to show how strong Invincible Girl was. Now the train is using her to show how invincible *it* is. It's using my story.

I can do that too. I remember what I wrote. "But you can't build the weapon without the help of the other scientists. And there's no one else here."

"I don't need them. You're going to build it for me."

She smiles.

"You seem like very good cooks."

Akio called us cooks too. Whatever we feed her, she takes. Our words, our wishes . . . our fears.

Akio shakes his head. He speaks too softly for the translator to pick up his words, but I think his lips say, "Very bad. Very bad."

Mariana speaks up. "We would . . . we would never build a weapon for you! You're a villain!"

Petra sticks out her bottom lip in a mock pout. "Oh, my dears, don't you see? You're as bad as I am. The Fear inside you, sly and strong, it feeds all of us. It fuels this train. You've already gathered the pieces of my weapon. We just need to build him. Are you ready? He's going to be magnificent."

Him? Who is she talking about?

Eleazar speaks up. "Not real," he says. "You're not real."

I grab his sweatshirt. "Don't provoke her."

But it's too late. She heard him.

Fide grins. "Not real? What exactly do you think I am? Some kind of fake? I'm as real as The Fear that stirs inside you.

But if you'd like, I can test your theory. Do you want to see how real I am?"

She lifts her blasters. Eleazar raises his fists. He's going to take another leap without thinking, like he did in the fake Medellín. And Fide's going to get him.

"No! Wait! A riddle," I cry, hoping that this Fide likes puzzles and clues as much as the villain I wrote about in the library car. "Give us a chance to stop you. Please."

My words feel a lot weaker than Invincible Girl's. Sometimes when I compare myself to her, I feel invisible. I wonder if I was even loud enough for Fide to hear me at all, but then she begins.

"All right, I'll give you one. But you shouldn't ever say *please* to someone like me. Do I look like I'm polite?"

"No, please—I mean . . ." I hold my chin up and try to make my words strong. "Just give us the riddle."

"Who walks on two legs but runs on four feet, died years ago but still begs for treats?"

Mariana looks my way. "Only people walk on two legs."

"And animals have four feet . . . ," I say.

Fide rests her blasters on top of her shoulders. "Tick-tock, tick-tock."

I ignore her and turn to Eleazar. "An animal who likes treats . . . dogs!"

He frowns. There's so much purple reflected in his eyes. "But my dog isn't dead. She can't be!"

"But the person she was named after is, right? I'm pretty sure she walked on two feet."

Eleazar nods and says, "Louisa May Alcott."

His face twists with rage, and he turns to Petra Fide. "Why is that your riddle? Do you have her?"

"She's in the engine room now," Fide says with a smirk. "Thanks to you all, it's burning strong. Don't worry, though, I'll keep her safe."

"No!" cries Eleazar.

"What about the Great Conductor?" Mariana asks. "Did you kidnap him, too?"

Petra Fide's smile widens.

My heart THWACKs inside my chest. *Louisa May Alcott has been trapped by Fide all this time?* And the Great Conductor was never waiting for us. It's a terrible, horrible thought, one that burns as badly as the purple smoke.

"We got the riddle," I protest. Angry tears burn behind my eyes. "You have to stop. Those are the rules that are—I mean, were—in my comics."

"Oh dear, you don't believe everything that happens in books, do you? I don't play by the same rules as your precious little villains. But thank you for telling me your weakness. It was very helpful."

Purple flames burst out of the ends of Fide's blasters. I look at Mariana. Fire should never have been a weakness.

But now it is.

Fide aims her blasters at the floor.

The train car trembles like we're standing on a giant electric toothbrush. The whole train car shakes with as much fear as I feel pulsing through my body. Pieces of glass and scrap metal bounce on the vibrating floor.

Eleazar runs toward the door after Fide, but as he moves through the earthquake of metal gears and wires, they rise into the air as though drawn toward the ceiling by an invisible magnet.

No, not toward the ceiling—toward one another. All the scraps in the room collide in a swirling storm. The gears fuse with flat pieces of metal, and wires spark as they twist themselves over and through the other pieces, tying and welding everything together until it takes the shape of a cannon.

Eleazar stops two feet from the door and stares at the cannon. It changes again. The scraps form another giant machine—no, not a machine, a *creature*.

A creature with wings made of broken glass, a mechanical tail, and sharp metal triangles of steel that run like spikes down its back.

That can't be what I think it is.

It's bigger than all four of us combined.

The metal creature turns on us.

We are too small for this.

Eleazar freezes in front of the door as Fide blasts her laser directly into the center of the beast, animating it with her purple cloud. Purple smoke and sparks ignite inside the gears and chains of the creature's chest.

I think of the riddle I left unanswered in my comic book.

What has two wings, green eyes, plays with fire, and never dies?

The creature is exactly what I think it is. *A dragon.*

Satisfied with her new weapon, Fide turns to leave.

"There's a storm coming your way," she says, pushing Eleazar aside. "And there's nothing you can do to stop it."

She disappears through the door.

The cloud inside the dragon's chest grows larger, rushing up through the beast's twisted neck. It turns toward Mariana.

"DUCK!" I shout. "NOW!"

Akio swoops in and skates in front of Mariana. The dragon focuses on him instead. Akio circles the train car in a bunch of complicated loops and figure eights. The dragon spins, trying to keep up with him. Eventually it throws its head back in frustration.

Purple flames with white-hot tips erupt from the dragon's mouth. The flames fly over my head, filling the train car with heat and smoke.

The dragon points its head toward the sky, and the flames

form glowing letters—BOOM—before blasting a hole through the ceiling.

My hands cover my mouth.

The purple smoke is thick and heavy in the air. I can't see the other side of the dragon; I can't see the door.

Mariana screams somewhere in the train car. Her cry is piercing enough to burst through the River of Allergies, but her words are mixed in with the screams.

Someone grabs my wrist. I catch a glimpse of orange through the smoke.

"Eleazar?" I say. He was so close to the door, I thought for sure he'd already be racing after Fide. He has all the courage in the world. But he stayed with us.

He pulls my wrist urgently.

I turn around as two round lights appear in front of my face, little light bulbs in the dark.

The dragon has its eyes on me.

I scramble backward, pulling Eleazar with me.

Some of the purple smoke blows over our heads and rises out of the hole the dragon made in the ceiling, clearing the air enough for me to see the dragon's body.

Another tumble of smoke and purple sparks builds inside its chest.

The gears on the dragon's metal mouth twist as it opens wide. Its sharp glass teeth reflect an eerie purple glow as I stare directly down the dragon's throat.

Flames build inside its mouth. I look at Eleazar. Our eyes meet, and I see that he's just as scared as I am.

Mariana crawls over to us. It's hard to see through all the smoke, but I see enough.

". . . your fault." I read her lips. She can't mean that.

"I'm not the one who said that Fide wins!" I cry.

Another burst of flames swoops overhead. Instinctively the three of us fall into a pile with our arms wrapped around one another. When the flames clear, we sit up, and I see another word on Mariana's lips.

Sorry. Over and over again. She didn't mean it. She's just scared. I say *sorry* too. But this is not my fault or hers. It's all the train.

Superstrength, I remind myself. We have superstrength.

But I don't feel strong at all. Eleazar gets up and prepares to run at the dragon. His knees are bent and his fists are raised. He has the sort of bravery that knights have in old books about slaying dragons. It's the sort of bravery I don't have.

But I made it across Barefoot Park for him, step by step, and I can handle this, too. There's a river in my head and a fire surrounding me, but I stick my chest out and keep my head up. I stand beside Eleazar and feel Mariana's shoulder against mine.

This is it. I know what we have to do.

We're gonna punch this dragon in the face.

CHAPTER
18

AKIO'S ROLLER SKATES leave marks on the floor as he dances around the dragon. He's still distracting it.

"Now!" I yell. I run as fast as I can. I can feel Mariana and Eleazar by my side, so close that our arms and elbows knock together. We crouch beneath the dragon and punch up into its jaw. Together the three of us knock the dragon's head backward. Bits of metal bend and snap, sending sharp pieces and blue sparks flying across the room.

The dragon screeches in pain. Its cry breaks through the River of Allergies and mixes with the sharp ringing in my ears.

The dragon flaps its metal wings and rises from the floor. It flies through the hole in the ceiling. Purple flames shoot out of the dragon's mouth as it escapes. It takes off into the sky, leaving behind a winding trail of purple smoke and flame that engulfs us.

The might of the dragon's final cry blurs my vision as the purple smoke surrounds me. It seems to fill me from head to toe. If my doctor wanted to take a sample of my blood, he'd find it stained purple. This is *The Fear* that Fide was talking about. Her weapon.

I feel a pain and tightness in my heart and lungs, as sharp as a needle, expanding in my chest like an unpoppable balloon. My breaths come short and fast, and it feels like I'm barely getting any air.

The THWACK-THWACK of my heart moves into my throat, and I choke.

THWACK-THWACK.

THWACK-THWACK.

Air. I need air. I tuck my head between my legs and try to breathe.

✝

I open my eyes. The air in the gym is mostly clear. Eleazar stands over me.

I see him say, "Okay?"

I nod. "Where's the fire? Where's the dragon?"

Eleazar fumbles with my phone, then hands it to me.

"The dragon flew out, and most of the smoke went out the hole too."

"Thank goodness," Mariana says.

Akio looks at me with some concern. He pulls three water bottles out of a hidden pocket in his jacket and hands them to us, then skates backward before we can thank him.

"I think I punched a dragon in the face," I say. The water is clear and cold and makes me feel instantly better.

Mariana and Eleazar give me cheesy, tired smiles. "We all did," Eleazar says.

"Oh no," Mariana says suddenly, her eyes on something along the wall. "My potatoes!"

Her backpack got hit by one of the flames. Eleazar retrieves it and dumps out the contents. The potatoes are crispy and charred, but they actually don't smell too bad. Eleazar holds one up to his mouth and takes a huge bite, then spits it out, sending dragon-fried potato flying across the room.

Mariana doubles over laughing. I manage a small smile. She looks up at me, and her face turns serious.

"I'm so sorry I took your book," she says. "It's all my fault. I didn't know your story was magical. I ruined it, and then it became real. I hope you still want to be my friend."

My eyes widen. I didn't know she wanted me to be her friend.

"It's okay," I say. "I . . . I still want to be your friend." After everything, the word *friend* feels bigger than it did before. Almost as big as the word *fear*.

Almost.

"Terrible cooks!" Akio says again. He shakes his head at the potatoes. Before, I thought he meant that we had bad wishes. But Fide said that our fear *fuels* the train.

"Akio, what does the engine run on?"

He points a finger at my chest.

THWACK-THWACK.

I look at Mariana and Eleazar. "That's what Fide said too.

And my train ticket. It said I paid for the ticket with fuel. Our fear fuels the train. If the engine is like an oven, then we're the cooks who decide which ingredients go inside."

I think about all the times I've been scared since we boarded—I was scared before I even made the first leap onto the train.

"It needs passengers to run," Eleazar agrees. "It needs our feelings or fuel or whatever."

"And if we're fueling it with fear, then it makes sense that the train is scary," I say.

"But," Mariana says, "that means that what's broken in the train isn't the engine. It's us."

I grimace. I don't want to think about it like that. It means the storms raging outside are our fault. Mom's texts say the storms have been getting worse ever since I got on the train—ever since the train got more passengers. But I remind myself we weren't here when the storms first started. We're not the only broken things. I take another sip of my water and look at Akio. He pretends not to like us, but maybe he was scared, being on the train all alone. I still don't know what made it start running again after so long, though.

"What about Louisa?" Eleazar asks. "Do you think she's scared too? She doesn't have us to keep her calm."

"I don't think The Fear affects animals," Akio says.

I blink away the tears filling my eyes at the thought of Louisa alone and afraid. I want to believe Akio. "How do you know?"

He reaches into his jacket pocket and pulls out a very tiny fish tank with an even tinier fish inside.

"Bernice isn't scared at all. When she's scared, she zooms around her tank. See, watch this."

He makes a scary face at the fish tank, and the little fish swims around in circles. When Akio's face softens, the fish calms down again.

"See? She was in my jacket when the dragon smoke filled the room, and it didn't bother her one bit."

It's hard to trust a man who keeps a very tiny fish in his pocket, but tiny Bernice's bravery gives me the tiniest bit of hope.

"If The Fear comes from us, then we can fight it," I say. "The train and Fide. If we stop being afraid, the train will have nothing to run on. Fide's not real. She's just a mix of magic and my fear. We can stop her."

"I'm not afraid," Eleazar says, but he looks at his feet. I know what he's not ready to say.

"I am," Mariana says.

"Me most of all, I fear." Akio hangs his head and tucks Bernice back inside his jacket.

The train took our wishes and our fears and turned them into storms and nightmares that made us even more afraid. *We fell for it.* We gave it so much fuel. Now our fear has turned into a dragon and a supervillain who won't stop until everyone is afraid. This isn't fair.

"It's not your fault." Mariana's words pop up on my screen. She's looking at Akio, but I think she's talking to all of us.

We're in this together now.

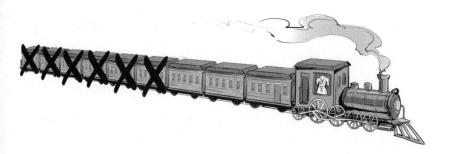

CHAPTER
19

WE STAND ON another platform connecting the train cars. Mariana said astronauts train for years to remain calm and unafraid under stress, but we could at least take some deep breaths to get rid of our fears before moving on to the next train car. I'm not sure deep breaths are working. My head spins and my eyes water. It feels like there's a war between my throat, my rebel stomach, and whatever tube connects them.

Grievance number eight billion. I keep my eyes shut tight and imagine Akio's notebook and the funny, loopy way he writes the letter G, but it's no use. I can't focus on the G enough to make my head stop spinning. Fide and her dragon are more than a grievance and more than regular fear.

They're nightmares.

I open my eyes again. The train races past small houses and short-stacked apartment buildings. We're on the north side of the city now. I wonder if this is where Mom comes to buy rainbow chard. The thought of her makes me breathe a little easier. She would tell me that it's okay to be sad and scared, that meeting a supervillain and facing a dragon is doing a little too much for one day. She would tell me to come home. If my research was right, we'll go to the end of one of the train lines and then turn around and head back for the Loop downtown, and home to the South Side after that.

No one on the streets looks up at us—their eyes are focused on something bigger. They're all staring at the southern sky.

The mechanical dragon flies out from behind a stretching skyscraper and shoots purple flames into the sky. They leave behind thick clouds of purple smoke that settle over the city. I wince. Mom and Dad are out there.

Fide's weapon is working.

Even though the dragon is far away, I can still feel the sting of The Fear in my lungs. The purple clouds of smoke left behind by the flames slowly fill the spaces between buildings. If the people down in the streets breathe in the smoke, they'll feel the same things I did—panic and choking and pain in their chests. They need a hero to save them—or heroes.

If we don't move quickly, we won't be able to stop Fide before The Fear takes over the city and we lose Louisa May Alcott—and everyone else—forever. It's time to take her down.

I try to make my heart stop pounding. Eleazar's eyes are screwed shut. He looks so focused that it makes me smile. *Oh.* That's better. The THWACK-THWACK of my racing heart slows down.

I'm ready.

A forest fills the next train car, but it doesn't look like any picture of a forest I've seen. The trees are eerie and strange, black from root to leaf, and so shiny that they don't seem real. Some of their branches connect over our heads. The spaces between the trees are dark and misty, so I can't see how far the forest spreads. I can't stare at them for more than a second before I start to feel like I'm swaying again—*or are the trees swaying?* I shiver.

The trees look like they've been charred black from a fire, but if that were true, the leaves wouldn't still be attached to their branches.

"Who wished for this?" Akio asks, but no one answers. Forests aren't my thing. But maybe . . .

"It was Fide," I say. "She must be hiding here somewhere. I'm going to find her."

I walk faster, but Eleazar stops me.

"Let's stick together," he says. A few train cars ago he would have been running ahead of me, not wanting to stay close. He must be able to read the surprise on my face, because his eyes narrow and he says, "I'm not afraid. It's smarter."

"Okay," I say. At least he admitted he wanted to stick together. "We have to try really hard not to be afraid."

Eleazar pushes his hair out of his face. "I already said I wasn't!"

He grabs my right hand. Mariana shuffles closer to us.

The forest floor is made of light, smooth stone like a fancy marble countertop. It's a strange contrast to the trees, but Akio skates over it easily, ducking under a few branches.

"There!" He points, and sure enough, I see her. A wisp of blue hair between the trees. We run after Fide, staying close together, going deeper and deeper into the forest, but she's always a few trees ahead. We can't catch her. Finally we reach a silver door. There are leaf-covered branches growing over it, tightening their grip around the handle with every second. Mariana tries to pull them off, but they're growing too fast.

"What happened?" Eleazar asks. "Is she gone?"

"She must have gone through the door," I say.

Mariana frowns at the branches on the door. "I think we're trapped."

Akio skates forward and picks up something from the floor—a paintbrush with a wood handle. The bristles are the same blue as Fide's hair. *Ugh.*

I raise an eyebrow at Eleazar and try to ask a question with my eyes. *Who would paint in a place like this?*

Akio rubs his thumb over the bristles on the paintbrush. He brushes the blue tip against one of the branches over the door, then kneels down to paint on the floor in long, delicate strokes.

My mouth falls open in shock. Eleazar points at my scared face and shakes his head. *Oh, right.*

"I'm not scared at all," I say, throwing back my shoulders.

"Me neither."

"Good."

"Good."

"Where's the paint coming from?" Mariana asks.

Akio paints big letters on the floor. *From the trees, of course.*

"They're . . . they're made of paint?"

I pinch one of the leaves between my fingers. It's delicate, as thin as the tissue paper we buy at Walgreens on Mother's Day. It breaks off easily and melts into dark goop that sticks to my thumb.

Akio keeps painting. *I think I've seen them before, but I can't remember. They're practically dried out. It must be ages since I was last here. . . .*

I take a step forward, and my arm brushes against a tree branch. A strange feeling fills me—of magic laced into the air like thousands of invisible branches. I think the trees have been sleeping for a long time, and now we're waking them up. *I want to get out of here.*

Then I remember I'm supposed to be fighting my fear, so I make my brain say something else. *This is great. It's a vacation. I've never been to Disney World, but now I can say I've been in a forest made of paint, which is cool. Really cool.*

"What are we supposed to do?" asks Eleazar.

I take pictures of Akio's words to translate into Spanish in case Eleazar wants to read both. My battery's down to 15 percent.

Akio paints, *If we want the paint to move and reveal the door, we have to use some of it up.*

Sure enough, as he paints, some of the branches shrink away from the door.

"Do you mean that if we keep taking paint from the trees, they'll shrink?" I ask.

"We'd better paint a lot," says Eleazar. "That door is really stuck."

"We could tell the trees a story," says Mariana.

"Not a scary one!" I remind them.

Good idea, Akio paints. *This is my story.*

Mariana's eyes light up.

Once upon a time, a man met a woman. Her name was Something or Other. Yes, that's right. The man and Something or Other fell in . . . well, they fell into a Place. Or perhaps they fell into an Abstract Concept. I'm not sure if they were hurt.

As he paints, the leaves and the branches begin to sway very gently, as though pushed by the gentlest breeze. More leaves fall away from the branches on the door.

They found a smaller person. I'm not sure where the Small One came from; perhaps it was delivered by a large bird. Anyway, something happened. The Thing That Always Happens Happened. And the woman was gone. But the man and the Small One remained.

They were terribly sad, I think. And they needed a way—

Akio pauses. The branches closest to him twist up and away.

"Keep going," I say.

But all he paints is, *I can't remember. I wish I could.*

He drops the brush, spraying dark paint across the floor. He doesn't have a finished story.

The trees aren't pleased. The branches stretch and twist

with quick, sharp motions. A twig wraps itself around Akio's wrist. He grimaces in pain—and fear.

"The trees didn't like his story," Mariana says. "What now?"

Akio uses his free hand to point at the paintbrush.

"We need to keep painting!" says Eleazar. "The brush is the only clue in here. There must be a way to tell the trees what they want."

I hold my phone in my left hand and grab the paintbrush with my right.

INVINCIBLE GIRL flies above a dark forest. She's looking for the one and only—

Eleazar taps my shoulder urgently. He points to his feet. Slimy roots slide through his shoelaces, tying him to the ground.

The forest doesn't like my Invincible Girl story either.

"How did you get it to work?" I ask Akio. There are branches around both of his wrists now. "The branches were moving away before you forgot the rest of the story."

"Tell the truth."

I frown. "The truth isn't a clue to be worked out. It's not a puzzle."

"It is for me," says Akio. He pulls half-heartedly at the branches wrapped around his wrists. "I can't remember all the pieces of my life."

I look down at the paintbrush in my hand.

It wants me to write something true. To put the pieces of me together, and not just the ones with Invincible Girl. It wants the pieces I'd rather keep hidden under a carpet. But I have to tell the truth without telling the *whole* truth. Because I can't include my fear.

When I found out I might have Ménière's disease, my doctor told me not to eat salt. I said, "But what about that label on the bottom of salt cans that says 'Iodine Is a Necessary Nutrient'?" He laughed and looked at my mom instead of me when he started listing all the other things I shouldn't do. I'm supposed to stay away from stress.

I turn around. The trees are shrinking again. Eleazar smiles, probably because staying away from stress on a magical train that might be trying to kill us is a ridiculous idea. But I'm still here, aren't I? His smile makes me feel a little bit more brave.

I keep painting.

There are so many things I'll have to be careful with in case I get dizzy, like learning how to drive a car or fly a plane or a spaceship.

I look up at Mariana, the astronaut-conductor. *Not that I want to be an astronaut when I'm grown, but it would be nice to have the option. Instead I'm stuck with a lifetime of being thrown around in a space camp simulator.*

The roots let go of Eleazar's feet, and the branches pull from the door even more. My story's working!

I pass the paintbrush to Eleazar.

He paints, *Extraño a mi abuela muchísimo. Odio Chicago. No volveré donde mi mamá. Regresaré a donde pertenezco.*

Before I can translate his words, he gives the paintbrush to Mariana.

The door is almost free. I bet Fide thought this would keep us busy for longer. We're still coming for her.

Mariana hesitates for several seconds before painting, *I'm alone. I have no one left.*

I almost stop her and tell her that she can't be alone because we're all right here, but I guess I know what it's like to feel invisible in a crowded place. I don't say anything.

Mariana continues, *Everything is wrong and broken. I'm afraid.*

"No! Mariana, what are you doing?"

"I'm sorry," she says. "But it's the truth."

She drops the brush. Paint splatters over my story, but I know I can't be mad at Mariana. I feel the same way she does. There's wrongness and brokenness and fear hidden in the spaces between every word I painted. I think the forest can sense it. The strange feeling I had before fills me again. Invisible branches tickle my neck, sending a prickle of fear down my spine.

The *f* in Mariana's *afraid* twists itself away from the other letters. It drips paint that forms new words. The train writes us another poem.

> *Fear is the spark that makes us run.*
> *Fear is our twisted, tangled fun.*
> *Doubt creeps up, the train takes flight.*
> *Watch the city fall to fright.*

> *If you find the engine boiling,*
> *Then successful was your toiling.*
> *Discover here your heart's desire;*

Keep it safe within the fire.

If you want to find what's lost,

Make a choice, then pay the cost.

Eleazar looks at me with wide eyes.

DRIP. DRIP. Big globs of paint smack against my forehead. The trees are melting. The branches covering the door fall away.

I lift my phone above the poem and take a quick picture.

My battery's down to 12 percent. It's already after three. I have another screenful of texts from Mom.

I need you to come home. I know Dad said 5:00 but the storms are getting too bad.

Come home right now.

Answer your phone!

Your location's off.

Etta, I need you. Please.

I'm scared.

I feel like I could throw up. I don't want Mom to feel what I'm feeling.

Indoors with Eleazar, I text back. Perfectly safe.

A big glob of paint falls onto the screen.

Eleazar points to the door. I run toward it. A giant branch collapses in a whoosh of paint that pours down my back.

I stop in my tracks. Horror fills me from head to toe.

The poem said *twisted, tangled fun.* It's so similar to the riddle I wrote for Fide in the train car with all the books: *What twists all your foolish dreams, tangles hopes, but is fun for me?* I never had a chance to come up with the answer before I fell asleep—*so the train did it for me.* I wanted to write about a supervillain in a made-up world who gets pummeled by Invincible Girl, not tell a true story that got me nothing but a head full of paint-splattered hair. At least we know we still need to get to the engine room.

The door is slick with paint. I claw at it until it opens.

Frustration makes my head throb. Fear keeps my ears ringing.

We make it out, but it doesn't feel like an escape.

Somewhere ahead, Fide is still waiting.

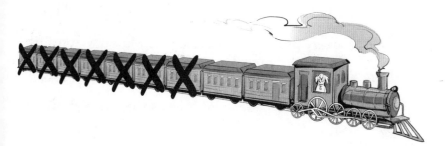

CHAPTER 20

"THERE! She's right there!"

We race into the next train car, but I catch only a glimpse of Fide before she disappears through another silver door. It vanishes with her.

"The train is toying with us," I say. "It's not listening to any wishes anymore."

If it were, Fide wouldn't be here at all. And it would have given me a battery pack so I could keep my Ms. Suzy app alive.

There are only two cars left before we reach the engine room. The floor is the same color blue as the space above us.

There are no walls or ceilings, just blue, blue, and more blue. I feel the rumbling of the train somewhere beneath us. A sense of dread fills me, like the uneasy feeling you get in the minutes before a math test or a doctor's appointment.

There must be something lurking here.

Something worse than dragons. It just hasn't revealed itself yet. Eleazar, Mariana, and Akio look scared too.

That's not good. But I don't know how to fight my own feelings. How are we going to beat Fide when we're still so afraid?

My eye catches on something on the ground, different from all that blue. Louisa May Alcott's collar! Eleazar's face crumples. Louisa is alone, held captive by Fide, with no collar to remind her where she really belongs.

Mariana picks up the collar and reads the words on the little sailboat before passing it to Eleazar.

"'I'm not afraid of storms, for I'm learning how to sail my ship.'"

She doesn't look like she isn't afraid.

Akio's eyes flash purple. "No! Not the storm!" he says.

He skates off into the distance. "Wait!" I cry. "What are you doing? There's nowhere to go."

My heart THWACKs. There's nowhere to hide. And no doors leading forward or back.

Akio doesn't turn back around. He skates and skates until his figure becomes a tiny, dark splotch in all the blue.

"What about the clue?" I ask, my heart sinking. "Where is it?"

Eleazar signs, "Confused."

Mariana looks unsure too. "Maybe we should follow Akio."

But I'm tired of running through all these train cars. And now, standing in this open space, it feels like we're farther away than ever from the end. But I nod and sign, "Run," because I don't know what else to do.

My feet don't get a chance to move. The storm comes from nowhere. It smacks me right in the face. A thick, swirling, sparkling cloud of purple fills the empty train car. I can't see through it at all.

It isn't just a storm. It's a wall. I try to move forward, but it pushes me back. I feel like one of those reporters on TV getting knocked over by a hurricane in Florida.

Rain pours through the clouds; smoke swirls over the ground.

I see shadows in front of me. *Eleazar and Mariana.* They

look weirdly tall. The storm clears just enough for me to follow them. I reach out my hand—but the shadows aren't solid. And they're not Eleazar or Mariana.

It's Mom and Dad.

I miss them so much.

I wipe away tears that come on hard and fast. My parents look like ghosts fading into the storm. The colors of their skin and clothes fade in and out of the purple. I follow them a little farther, into a strange, blurred version of my house.

Dad sits down at the table. His internet browser is pulled up. He has a bunch of websites open, and they're all about me.

Ménière's disease triggers.

Ménière's disease diet.

"Dad, stop googling that stuff!" I say, but they can't hear me. I'm not really in the house with them. Mom's staring at her phone. I pull mine out of my pocket. Nine percent. There's no service in the storm. I can't send Mom any more texts telling her I'm safe. *She must be so afraid.*

Dad shuts the laptop and puts his head into his hands. He doesn't move for a long time.

My heart THWACKs. I didn't mean to make my parents this upset.

Mom wrings her hands. A wisp of purple steam rises from Dad's plate of Fanksgiving leftovers. He starts coughing and clutching at his chest. He looks as stricken as I felt when I breathed smoke from the dragon.

Dad wanted me to be brave. He thought I had a little fight in me.

I'm not sure I ever did. Now he's filled with The Fear too.

He waves at my mom frantically, and she gets up to shut the window, but it's too late. The storm is already inside. Purple clouds overtake them, and then they're gone. *No!*

"Mom! Come back!" I cry. I push my way through the storm, looking for any sign of her, but it's no use. She's gone. I don't want her to feel The Fear I'm feeling; I just want her to feel my hand in hers.

I cry out for Eleazar and the others, but even if they are in here, somewhere, the only sound that fills my ears is a high-pitched ringing.

Heroes are supposed to beat their villains. But Invincible

Girl's story is over. In the end, she was just as afraid of Fide as I am.

I need to focus on something solid and steady before dizziness takes control.

I shut my eyes and slide down to the floor. I try to focus on pictures in my head—an empty comic book panel, Dr. Petra Fide's lab coat, arepas—but they all get twisted and blurry, just like everything else on the train.

The ringing in my ears screeches as loud as an ambulance, but there's no help coming.

Breathe. I need to breathe.

I take deep breaths in and out, trying to push all The Fear out of my lungs. I hate this feeling. It's like my body doesn't belong to me.

I grit my teeth. This is the part of the story where Superman finds a way to get rid of his Kryptonite. But how can I get rid of something that's inside me?

I wait with closed eyes and closed fists until the dizziness calms. The storm still rages on. I don't know how long I sit.

A memory of Mom floats into my head as the dizziness

starts to clear. Not storm-ghost Mom. *Real* Mom. She bought me my first-ever sketchbook. Actually, I think it was supposed to be a diary, but I used it to make comics. I tried to draw Spider-Man and She-Hulk and Black Panther, but none of my pictures looked like the ones in real comics. Mom told me I needed to stop copying others and make my own path.

My own heroine.

That's when I started drawing Invincible Girl.

Finally I feel steady enough to open my eyes.

I think of my parents' faces in the storm. I can't sit by and watch while fear breaks the strongest people I know.

I have to fix this.

I know my fear is fueling the train.

Just stop being afraid, Etta Johnson. Stop. My heart THWACKs harder.

Nowhere is safe.

Dragons behind me, Fide ahead.

It feels like The Fear has surrounded us for so long.

I remind myself that the train was once good. That's what Mariana said. Maybe that means there's another kind of fuel that exists alongside the fear. After all, the train didn't create an impossible maze. There was a way to get through every train car, even when things went wrong. It could have trapped us, but it didn't. I hold on to that tiny piece of knowledge, that some small part of the train might be pushing back against The Fear that fills it.

I don't know how to be fearless. But I can try my best to be brave.

Mom's words enter my brain again.

Make your own path. I stand up slowly and focus only on the feel of the ground beneath my feet. My hands don't stop shaking, but my right foot follows my left, and then the left scoots forward again. I remember my fists going through all those punching bags—*right, left, right*—as I put one foot in front of the other. Maybe for me, being strong doesn't mean being invincible.

Maybe it's just a heavy foot followed by a heavy foot followed by hope.

Another shadow appears by my right side.

Eleazar! And he's not a storm ghost. I know because I bump

right into him. Close up, I can see his hair blowing around his face, but I can't read any words coming off his lips. I grab his arm, and we try to push against the storm together.

I wish we still had our superstrength, but it's no use.

The Fear enters my chest and sends everything spinning again. I choke as it surrounds my face and burns its way into my lungs. My stinging eyes water down my face. Another shape knocks into my back, and I fall over, bringing Eleazar down with me.

It feels like I'm running out of air.

Just an inch, I tell myself. I just need to make it forward one inch at a time—to push back against The Fear and find the good again.

I use all my strength to crawl forward with my arms.

Just one inch.

And suddenly the storm is gone. Or rather, I'm in the middle of it, and in the middle of it . . . there's nothing.

Just Quiet. Mariana and Eleazar crawl into the Quiet behind me.

It's a small circular space in the middle of the swirling storm.

All around us, The Fear continues to rage, but we're safe.

I think I'll stay here for a while.

My stomach flops back into place. The ringing in my ears fades, bringing me back to Quiet.

I breathe easier. *Okay.* After a few more breaths I turn on my phone. Four percent.

"It's an eye," says Mariana, looking around. "Like the eye of a hurricane."

"How do we get out?" Eleazar asks.

Mariana shakes her head. "I don't think you do. My mom showed me this story about birds who got trapped in the eye of a hurricane. They just had to stay there, moving with the hurricane, until it stopped."

"But then it'll be too late," I say. "Fide will have taken control of Chicago and moved on to somewhere else. Who knows where we'll end up? We won't be able to get home."

I stop talking. I'm not sure they care about getting home as much as I do. I look at the stuff spilling out of Eleazar's bag. Clothes and books and a toothbrush. And Mariana had all her potatoes before they got burnt up.

They don't care about getting home at all.

We sit in silence for a few minutes, watching the storm rage around us.

"Did you see anything in the storm?" I ask finally. "I think I saw my parents. But they looked like ghosts."

Mariana crosses her arms over her chest and shivers. "I saw something that couldn't possibly be real."

She doesn't say anything else.

Eleazar gives me a sad, empty stare. "I saw my grandma. She was walking Louisa in the mountains near Medellín. I miss all the green from home."

"No creepy paint trees there?"

He smiles. "Not a single one."

"I know it doesn't make any sense," he says. "Grandma never met Louisa. We got her when we moved here. But I wanted it to be real."

I take my backpack off my shoulders and pull my books out. They're sticky and covered with paint from the trees, but the copy of *Little Women* that I took from the train has a few unstained pages. I open it carefully and skim until a word catches my eye.

Castle.

A girl named Jo is talking about how fun it would be if all the castles in the air that the characters dream about were real. Someone named Laurie wants to have lots of music in their castle, Meg wants a lovely house with pretty clothes, and Beth is content to stay at home. But Jo wants something different.

I read out loud.

"'I'd have a stable full of Arabian steeds, rooms piled high with books, and I'd write out of a magic inkstand, so that my works should be as famous as Laurie's music. I want to do something splendid before I go into my castle, something heroic or wonderful that won't be forgotten after I'm dead. I don't know what, but I'm on the watch for it, and mean to astonish you all some day.'"

One of my big, fat tears falls onto the page.

The castles in the air don't sound so different from the worlds Invincible Girl visits. Jo wants to write too, and she even talks about rooms full of books.

Eleazar and I had the same wish—we both wanted the train car with the library and the warm snow.

But fear twisted it, and now we've lost control.

I read farther down the page.

"''I've got the key to my castle in the air, but whether I can unlock the door remains to be seen,' observed Jo mysteriously.'"

"We're missing the key," I say. "We need to find it. Then we can finish all of this and go home."

At the word *home*, Eleazar flinches.

"I have to tell you something," he says.

I look right into his serious, sad eyes. He looks away and pulls at the piece of hair in front of his face. I think I know what he's going to say.

Eleazar gestures to himself, then to *Little Women*, and then to a place far away in the sky. I see a glimmer of purple reflect off the whites in his eyes.

"I told you Louisa was my best friend, and she is, but before I moved here, I had another best friend. It's probably not who you think. It's my grandma."

I smile. I can't help it. First his grandma, then Louisa May? Eleazar has good taste in best friends.

"She's so cool. Every year on her birthday we do something special, but Mom said we were too busy to go visit this year. That's why I left your parents' house. You were talking about grandmas, and I got upset. I thought maybe with the magical train, I could take Louisa and go anyway. But now I lost her. I lost everything."

The castles in the sky—he doesn't want to build them here. He wants to go home.

Eleazar's face starts to spin as another wave of vertigo turns my stomach upside down. At least he told me. I should be honest with him, too.

"I have to tell you something too," I say. "I have Ménière's disease—"

"I saw you paint that," he says. "I didn't know what it meant. Are you going to die?"

"No," I say. "But there's no cure. I could never be an astronaut."

Eleazar looks at the ground. My heart THWACKs, and my ears ring.

My battery's down to 2 percent. And we have less than an hour to make it home before Dad's curfew. If there were service in this train car, I bet I'd have a thousand texts from Mom.

Eleazar rubs his finger over a splotch of paint on his shoe.

"I wish I could tell my grandma about this. She'd never believe me. This is weirder than any of her stories."

"What about your mom?" I say. "Does she tell stories?"

He shrugs. "Not as many."

"My mom is really, really worried about me. She'd be so mad if she knew I ate an arepa."

Eleazar half smiles.

Mariana cuts in. Her words appear on my screen slowly.

"I have a secret too. I came here because I had nowhere else to go. Because my mom is . . ."

Oh no.

"She's dead. She passed away three years ago. Her name was Keiko, and she was kind and beautiful. I've been living with my auntie. But two weeks ago I was looking through a box of Mom's old stuff and found the map she made for me. It had money to get here from St. Louis on the Amtrak train, instructions to my great-aunt's house in Chicago, and clues about how to find this train. Mom said I would find the Great Conductor and everything would be okay. Even my auntie and my great-aunt said the conductor would be waiting for me. . . . I'm worried that the things they told me about the train were never true. There's no Great Conductor. There's no one waiting for me."

My eyes fill with tears. I feel horrible. My mom is worried and Eleazar's mom is busy, but they're still here.

I ask, "Did you know your mom was—"

"I knew she was sick. I didn't know it would be over so soon. I didn't get to say goodbye." She wipes away a tear. "Did you know you were sick?"

"I knew about the Quiet first," I say. "I didn't know about the dizziness and the ringing or that there was no cure. It doesn't feel good. If you ever go to space, I won't be coming with you."

I don't know what else to say, but I feel a terrible, aching sadness that burns from the corners of my eyes to the tips of my toes. Is there any word in the whole world sad and sorrowful and gentle enough to tell someone you wish their mother weren't dead? *Sad* sounds too harsh, even in my head, and *sorry* ends in *y*. It makes me want to ask Mariana, or the train, or anyone who knows the answer: *Why?* Why do hard things happen?

I blink fast. I feel so many THWACKs. One in my heart

for Eleazar, one in my head for the maybe-diagnosis, one for Mariana's mom, and one deep down in the bottom of my stomach, hanging out around the shards of my broken courage jar—for The Fear that spreads.

"Maybe it's not too late," I say, though I'm not sure I'm talking loud enough for them to hear me. "We never found our treasures, but that poem said your heart's desire was in the engine room. Maybe Eleazar could still go home, and Mariana could . . . she could . . ."

I stop. Eleazar and Mariana look doubtfully at the wall of purple smoke surrounding us.

"We'll find a way to get past it," I say, but my confidence wavers, and my words tumble over one another.

Even Ms. Suzy doesn't understand me. The app reads, "We ferret a wave to get pasta."

Eleazar raises his eyebrow at me.

I ignore the heat in my face and the ringing in my ears and try to talk more slowly.

"We'll make it through."

Eleazar turns Louisa's collar over in his hands.

I'm not afraid of storms, for I'm learning how to sail my ship.

"Mariana, when you said *storms*, Akio ran," I say. "Maybe the collar summoned the storm. So maybe it also has the clue to get us out."

"But we don't have a ship," says Mariana. "There's no boat here like in the other train car."

"And remember what Fide said," adds Eleazar. "She said the storm was coming, and there was no way to stop it."

They're right. We're stuck.

The phone dies. My mind goes as blank as the screen. All my hopes and ideas are gone.

"Sorry," I say, but I'm sure my words are coming out too soft.

Is this it? Is this as far as we go? We're so close to the last piece of the story, but it's still on the other side of the wall.

I look across the eye of the storm at Eleazar. He looks back. In the space between us, I see Louisa's cotton-candy fur. I see the color of the best caramel I've ever tasted and the story we could have written together. I see a punching bag flying across the room and a story painted on the ground. I don't know what's good and what's bad or how to save the things that matter.

I don't think he knows either.

My heart longs for my sketchbook. I want to write about Invincible Girl and let all the THWACKs and Fear disappear in my story. But it's covered in paint now. And Invincible Girl's story is over.

It doesn't matter. I may not have a sketchbook, but I still have my brain. I can imagine what the comic would look like.

The train can't take Invincible Girl away from me. I don't care how messed up or broken my comic became. Maybe being broken—or being unbreakable—aren't the most important things.

Even if Invincible Girl had a million weaknesses and was allergic to water, she'd still be my hero. She'd keep fighting.

INVINCIBLE GIRL LOOKS OVER A MAP OF A SPACE STATION AND AN UNDERGROUND LAIR.

INVINCIBLE GIRL: THESE SUPERHERO TEAMS SURE HAVE SOME STRANGE NAMES. BUT THERE ARE SOME FIGHTS EVEN I CAN'T WIN ALONE. I NEED A SQUAD.

SUPER QUASI-UNDERCOVER ADVENTURE DREAM TEAM.
OKAY, SO I GUESS WE'LL BE A SQUADT.

Next to me Mariana reaches out and places her hand in mine. She does the same to Eleazar, and then . . . he does the same to me.

The three of us hold hands in a little triangle in the middle of the storm. We sit in silence.

For a moment, Quiet is more than the absence of sound. It's more than whispers and the River of Allergies. It's a space, small but steady, that surrounds us. It's the fingers holding tight to mine. It's Peace.

The purple clouds almost seem to move back a few inches, as though someone blew a super-powerful breath at The Fear and pushed it away. A thin cloud colored blue and yellow fills in the gaps.

Together we're forming a different kind of ship. The kind that comes from sharing secrets; the kind that's as heavy as the word *friend*.

Maybe it's heavy enough to push through the storm like a battering ram from old stories about wars. Fide said there was no way to stop the storm; she didn't say we couldn't fight our way through it. I stand up without letting go of Eleazar's and Mariana's hands.

They stand with me. Without saying a word, we shut our eyes and shuffle sideways, right into the storm.

We push forward. The storm pushes back, but it doesn't break our triangle. We store a little bit of the eye's Quiet in the space between us.

We keep pushing until a door appears in the middle of the storm. I think that we made our own clue and our own key. We're the pieces of a puzzle.

Only, we're still missing a few passengers.

One more train car. Then we find Akio. Then we get Louisa back.

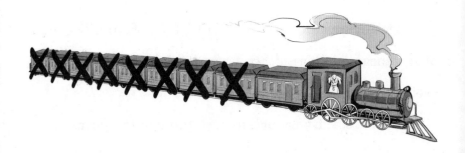

CHAPTER
21

I DON'T SEE Fide in the next train car, or a painted forest, or a dragon or a storm, or any of the things I thought we'd have to face. But I do see Louisa May Alcott.

Before I know it, Eleazar is on the floor, and Louisa May Alcott is on top of him. Her tail wags so hard that her whole body moves, and her cotton-candy fur is as fluffy as ever. A few feet behind them I see Mariana's outline, but Eleazar and Louisa are moving around too much for me to see anything more. I smile.

"Louisa! I can't believe you're here!" I cry. Eleazar throws his head back and laughs as she licks his face.

I reach out my hand to scratch Louisa's ears, but she turns and snaps at me. I pull my hand away quickly, but her ears flatten on her face and she snarls. She's not the friendly dog who sat next to me on the bus anymore.

Eleazar gives me an apologetic look.

"Sorry," he says. "She's not usually like this. She's probably nervous from being trapped for so long."

Eleazar's words appear in small subtitles beneath his chin. *Whoa.* The letters look like the pasta from alphabet soup, but when Eleazar swats at them, they vanish like a cloud.

"That's so cool," I say. It's even better than the magical app. My own words appear under my chin. I duck around them so I can get a good look.

"They're in Spanish!" I say, but Eleazar's too busy hugging Louisa May Alcott to pay attention to me. She snuggles her nose into his chest. She looks so clean—too clean, almost, like she spent this whole time getting a bath and a haircut. Meanwhile I'm covered in paint and bits of gummy worm.

"I can't believe she's here," I say. "It feels too—"

"Awesome!" Eleazar grins. "It's awesome. We finally made it."

"But we haven't reached the engine room yet. There's still one train car to go."

Eleazar laughs as Louisa burrows her head into his armpit. "Etta, this *is* the engine room. Look!"

He points to a table along the far wall of the train car. It's covered in letters and knobs and different-colored buttons. Above it, there's a neon flashing sign that says, *Welcome to the Engine Room.* I frown.

"That can't be right. There's supposed to be one more train car," I protest, but I don't feel confident. It *has* been a long day. Maybe we counted wrong.

Louisa nuzzles her nose against Eleazar's cheeks. "There might be another room," he says as he wraps his arms around her body. "But I bet you can't go in there. You wouldn't sit in the hood of a car engine, would you? This is obviously where all the engine controls are. And Louisa's here! So we're in the right place."

I look at the neon sign again. *Welcome to the Engine Room.* "But even if this is the engine room . . . don't you think it's weird that Fide isn't here? And where's Akio? I hope he's not still lost in the storm."

Eleazar shrugs. "Akio's probably back in his boat. But The Fear is gone. I don't feel it anymore. So Fide's probably gone too."

I think he's wrong.

There's a purple gleam in Eleazar's eyes.

"The Fear is still here. I . . . I think it might be inside you," I say.

"What? Why would you say that about me?"

"Your eyes—"

"I finally got Louisa back. How could I still be afraid?"

"I don't know. I don't have all the answers. I'm just—"

"You're just mad that Louisa doesn't like you."

I open my mouth to protest. But Louisa growls, and my voice falters.

"Give her some space," Eleazar says, holding her close. "You're scaring her. Maybe The Fear's inside you, not me."

I don't know. He's probably right. I turn to find Mariana— but she's already standing next to someone.

"This is my mom!" cries Mariana. "She's been waiting for me here all this time."

Subtitles appear beneath Mariana's chin too.

"Your *mom*?" I say. The woman's head is turned away from

me, but I still can't believe I didn't notice her standing there by Mariana. I miscounted the train cars, and now this . . . My head feels like it belongs to someone else.

The woman turns around to face me when I speak. She doesn't look like Mariana at first. Her straight black hair is pulled back into a bun, and she's wearing a long green coat. She has lighter skin and eyes than Mariana, but when I look closely, I see that a lot of their other features are the same.

But the train can't bring people back from the dead. *Can it?*

I watch Mariana and her maybe-mom, and Eleazar and Louisa. I feel a little left out. What was my heart's desire? Why isn't it here? All I have are my paint-stained books. But as I swing my backpack around, I see that it isn't covered in paint anymore. It looks like it just got washed. My fingers tremble as I open the zipper. My green sketchbook isn't there—there's something else in its place. It's a book. *A real book.* It has a shiny, colorful cover with a drawing of Invincible Girl on it.

Invincible Girl Rules the World

By Etta Johnson

Inside, the pages are filled with bright, colorful comics

and bold letters. The story looks exactly how I've always pictured it in my head. I can't believe it. This is my treasure. My heart's desire. And it's even better than the book it replaced. It's perfect. I can't read the pages quickly enough. The story is so good—Invincible Girl kicking butt all over town. I need to get home to show this to Mom.

Mom. I blink three times. Am I really on page 87 already? It feels like I've only been sitting here for a minute, but much more time must have passed. My phone is dead, so I can't see if Mom's been texting. Eleazar and Louisa are still hugging, and Mariana and her mom are chatting. They're in the exact same positions they were in when I started reading. Something's not right here. Petra Fide didn't even show up in this new story. Why would she disappear?

This is all starting to feel like a trap. I put the book in my backpack and explore the rest of the engine room. The door at the back didn't disappear when we entered, but I don't want to go into the storm again. There must a clue in the engine room. All the train's poems told us to come here. This car is as narrow as a normal train car, but much longer. The walls are lined with small television screens, each one playing a different movie. Most of the scenes are of kids doing different things. There's a girl sitting in the middle of a classroom, a boy on a stage in front of hundreds of people, and twins in front of a house that looks like it's on fire. Their names are written in the corners of the screens.

There are two tables in the room—one in the middle and the control table along the far wall that Eleazar pointed out earlier.

The first table is covered in food. It looks like a giant Fanksgiving feast, plus all of Eleazar's favorite foods. Probably Mariana's too. I back away, thinking about how much salt I ate earlier, but the smell of the food doesn't make me feel sick. *It smells wonderful.* I escape the temptation of more arepas and move toward the other table.

There are lots of small clocks and keyboards and meters, but I don't understand the numbers and symbols on them. One of the meters reads, DANGER LEVELS. There are five settings: IT'S ALL GOOD; THINGS ARE MOSTLY OKAY; START WORRYING; PRETTY BAD; and VERY DANGEROUS, INDEED.

The pointer is floating above VERY DANGEROUS, INDEED.

There *is* something wrong here. I knew it. I've got to figure out how to fix the train before Fide comes back.

There's a map behind one of the keyboards. It reads,

DESTINATION: CHICAGO

NEXT STOP: ERROR

The train is stuck on Chicago. My heart beats a little bit faster. I'm glad the train isn't going anywhere else, but the thought of it going round and round in circles spreading Fear in my city makes me feel scared—which means I'm fueling the train again.

Behind the maps and meters there's a clear container with pieces of black coal strewn across the bottom. Different-colored flames rise up from the coal. Most of the flames are purple, but a few spark blue and yellow and green. I remember the thin blue-and-yellow cloud that helped us escape the purple storm in the last train car. Those other colors must be the good part of the train. Maybe there's something here that pushes back against The Fear. Can the train run on something else, if it doesn't have our fear? I'm not sure it matters now. There's so little blue and yellow there.

Smoke from the flames rises above the coal and enters glass pipes that stretch up to the ceiling before disappearing into a series of metal pipes. I bet the pipes go through whatever machine is in the final train car and out the smokestack.

These are the same flames that came out of Fide's laser blasters. This must be where her power comes from. It's the storm inside us—come to life.

The coal is next to another glass container. This one has bubbling liquid on the bottom, with steam rising up from the surface. The steam has a few different colors too—the same as the fire in the coal—and more glass pipes connect the steam to a system beneath the train.

The poem said, *If you find the engine boiling, then successful was your toiling.* But it doesn't seem like our toiling and troubles are over. The Great Conductor isn't here to tell us what to do. Akio isn't even here. My heart THWACKs.

I didn't mean to leave him behind in the storm. I clench my fists. Hopefully he'll be okay for just a little while longer, until we can fix the train and save him.

We have to find a way to move the pointer from VERY DANGEROUS, INDEED to the other side so we can stop The Fear before Fide shows up.

I push some of the buttons and turn a few knobs, but nothing happens.

"Hey, over here! I need help!" I call out. I look back at the others, but Eleazar is busy hugging Louisa, and Mariana's eyes are fixed on her mom.

Mariana and her mom sit down at the table laden with food, and Eleazar joins them. Louisa puts her paws up on the table and licks out of a gravy bowl. Mariana beams at me.

"All this time I thought I was looking for the Great Conductor, but . . ." Her chest rises and falls, rises and falls. "It's her. She's the reason why I'm here."

Her mom extends her hand to me. Her fingers are long and delicate, and there's perfect red nail polish on them. They seem like the hands of a real person. But they're not.

They can't be. I take her hand. It's cold to the touch, even though the engine room is hot from the boiling liquid and smoke.

"Etta, dear," Mariana's mother says. My eyes narrow at the subtitles floating beneath her face. I am *not* this woman's dear. The only person allowed to call me dear is my mom, and she doesn't because that would be weird.

"I'm Keiko," the woman continues. "Nice to meet you. Thank you for sticking with Mariana on her long journey from our old home to the train. You helped bring her to me."

"Where is your old home?" I'm asking Keiko to see how much she knows, but Mariana answers.

"St. Louis. I told you, Etta, I took the Amtrak train to Chicago. Mom, you won't believe it: after I got to Great-Aunt Lilly's house, I followed your map to a train station, but I didn't see the train. Then I noticed the storms on the television and I saw the fireworks and I figured it all out. I remembered the stories you told me and tracked the train down."

"That's very clever, dear," says Keiko. She reaches out and pulls Mariana toward her, kissing her cheek.

I look at the dog sitting next to them. She growls at me again. *She isn't Louisa.*

She's another distraction, like the food stands and the books that made us fall asleep. She's a fake. Keeping us away from the VERY DANGEROUS, INDEED engine.

"Let's eat!" calls Mariana. "Come on, we can have a party to celebrate getting here!"

I open my mouth to protest, then pause. If I'd lost my dog or my mom, I might settle for a fake version too.

"We fueled the train; now we need fuel!" Mariana laughs, rubbing her belly.

"Mariana, we fueled the train with fear," I remind her. "I think it's still broken. And we left Akio—he might still be lost in the storm."

She shrugs. "The poem said, 'If you find the engine boiling, then successful was your toiling.' Looks like it's boiling to me."

She grins. Keiko laughs with her. Her smile is wide, but her eyes don't have any warmth in them. Keiko stares at a pitcher on the table for way too long. Her eyes blink. Blink. Blink. Too fast.

I point at the engine. "No, look at all the purple smoke. It's The Fear. The storm is still affecting the city . . . and us."

I look around, eyes smarting, trying to find a way to prove to them that this isn't right. Eleazar, at least, gets up and walks over to look at the engine. I move to join him, but Mariana calls out to me again. "Etta, let's have some cake!"

"What an excellent idea!" Keiko says. She's still staring at the pitcher. "Etta, my dear, do you want a small piece or a large piece?"

"I don't want any piece."

"Oh, you're so funny. Large pieces for everyone!" Keiko picks up a knife and presses it into the cake. She rocks it back and forth like she's slicing a turkey, not a soft cake. And she doesn't notice her own finger in the way.

"Uh-oh, Mom. Are you okay?" Mariana asks. The floating subtitles bounce around like they're not sure either.

"I'm doing wonderful, dear. How are you?"

"You're not wonderful. You're bleeding!" I say. I need to get out of here.

Keiko holds up her finger. There's a small cut on it, slowly dripping red onto the cake.

"Can't you feel that?" I ask.

"Of course not. There's no pain in the engine room."

"Yes there—" I start, but then I notice. I have no headache. My ears aren't ringing, and the upside-down feeling in my stomach is gone. In fact, I think the River of Allergies might be starting to clear up.

"You feel better, don't you?" Keiko asks. She offers me a piece of blood-stained cake, which I refuse. "You should be grateful."

I read her words and realize what she thinks I've gained. What the train thinks it gave me—and honestly, *how dare it?*

None of this is real. It's not possible, and it's *not me*. I feel a surge of regret. My maybe-diagnosis isn't like Kryptonite. It's not a magical alien rock that makes me weak. I don't need to run from it or crush it into bits. It's just me.

I'm so angry that my hands form fists, and I can't stop them from shaking. I'd rather be dizzy-Etta than never-Quiet-not-me-Etta. I don't want Ménière's disease to take control of my body, but that doesn't mean it's not a part of my story. I can't just erase it and replace it with a new story. *Oh no.* The stories in my sketchbook. My scratch-outs and my rewrites—they were part of me. I can't believe I was embarrassed to show them to Mom.

I stand up straight. I was and am as afraid as the others, but that doesn't mean I need to change. After all, I made it out of the storm. I held their hands when we thought all was lost.

I was strong enough to make it through the train cars.

But I don't know if I'm strong enough for this—for friends who don't see the real me.

"This is better, isn't it?" Keiko asks. There's a spark of life in her eyes now. She's mocking me. "What a wonderful life we'll have!"

"A *life*? What do you mean?"

Mariana claps. "It's not an engine. It's more like a home, right?"

They want to stay here. Forever.

I turn back to the engine. Eleazar stands in front of the control table, but he isn't trying to fix the pointer. His hands are on the keyboard below the map. He's typing—changing our destination.

Now the map reads, *NEXT STOP: MEDELLÍN*.

No! Why would he do that?

My head is full of whys. I want very badly to go home. I'm sorry that I ever came. The "gifts" we found in the engine room aren't wishes, not like apples or superstrength. They're not things that make you feel better, like doctors and medicine and holding the hand of someone you trust. These are *cures*. For homesickness. For disease. For death.

There's not supposed to be a cure for being who you are. The story that replaced my sketchbook feels cheap now. I didn't write it. And I can't show any of my work to Mom if I never leave this train.

My heart aches for her. She needs me. The dragon's still out there. How could Eleazar and Mariana forget that?

I try to wrap my head around the second poem again. *If you want to find what's lost, make a choice, then pay the cost.*

This is the price we have to pay to get these so-called gifts. We have to let The Fear take over Chicago. We have to stay here forever. *I don't want to pay.* But maybe Eleazar and Mariana do.

I think about Mariana's mom again, and Eleazar's grand-mother.

I don't know how it feels to lose a mother or live far away from the place that feels like home. It must be worse than anything I can imagine.

But I do know how it feels to be the quietest kid at every party and to write about heroes but never have friends. I know what it's like to feel stuck and alone. I join Eleazar by the engine controls.

"Look, Etta, we can go anywhere we want! It's going to take me home."

He sees the look on my face. "Etta, are you okay? We could just go visit for a little while, and then we'll come back. I promise."

Keiko appears behind us with Mariana. "I think that's an *excellent* idea. We can have a grand adventure together. Now how about this: Mariana will be the Great Conductor's apprentice—"

"There is no Great Conductor," I say.

"Well, then, seeing as how I am the only adult, I will take on that role."

"And you were an apprentice, so you already know every-thing," Mariana adds.

"Oh yes, that's right. I was an apprentice." Keiko sucks the cut on her finger. "Eleazar will be Master of the Maps, and . . ."

She looks down at me.

"How about you, dear? What role do you want?"

"I want to fix the engine," I say stubbornly.

"Perfect! An engineer. Just what we needed."

I don't return her smile. "If you're the conductor, then maybe you should do something about *that*."

I point to VERY DANGEROUS, INDEED.

Keiko ignores me. She looks back at her daughter.

The TV screen across from me flickers. A boy in one of the videos pauses in the middle of giving some speech to a huge crowd and throws up off the side of the stage.

He runs off. *That wasn't very brave.*

I don't feel brave either. This is all wrong.

I stand in front of the TV screen. It flickers, and then shows me my mom, just like the storms did. She's on the floor of her studio, surrounded by clouds. I take a step back and squeeze my head between my hands. My world is spinning again. But it's not from vertigo. It's spinning out of my control.

I need Eleazar to see that we haven't really saved anyone yet. I need an ally.

"Eleazar, please. I need to show you something."

"I'm very busy," he says. He's scratching Louisa's belly. *Dog people are weird.*

"Please," I say. I make my voice as serious as possible. "You trust me, right?"

He looks up and meets my gaze.

I point at the TV screen. The video changes again—this time it shows Eleazar's mom. She's looking at an older woman on a phone screen.

The old woman looks just like his mom.

Eleazar's grandma.

"Shh!" cries Eleazar. He runs over and leans in close to the TV. I read the subtitles that pop up on the screen.

"I miss you so much," says Eleazar's mom. "And Eleazar is miserable. I haven't even seen him since this morning. Did you know Louisa ran away? I'm so worried. Maybe we should have come back for your birthday."

"I raised you to be stronger than this!" Eleazar's grandma scoffs. "Anyone who has to go a day without seeing my beautiful face gets depressed, of course, but you can do it. And I throw the best parties, so I understand the tragedy of missing it. But now I know how to use FaceTime, so you can see me every day!"

Eleazar's mom nods. "Only two more months until the summer trip, I guess."

Eleazar looks confused.

"I'll make him the biggest surprise Spider-Man cake he's ever seen," says his grandma. Then she scratches her nose, and her expression goes from cheery to worried.

"What's wrong?" asks his mom.

His grandma frowns. "Smells like anise. And smoke."

"You really shouldn't be watching that," interrupts Keiko. She smacks the TV. Purple static covers the screen.

"No!" cries Eleazar. He hits the screen again, but the video doesn't come back. He looks at me with wide eyes. "She could smell the smoke. The Fear is headed for my grandma, too. I need to go home and warn my mom."

He blinks three times fast, just like I did after I realized I needed to go home. I think he's back on my side.

I nod. "If we go to Colombia now, we'll only bring The Fear with us," I say.

Eleazar hits the delete button on the keyboard with so much force that I think his finger will fall off. *MEDELLÍN* disappears from the *NEXT STOP* line.

Louisa May Alcott turns on him immediately. Her lips pull back over her teeth. Her fluffy fur trembles as she snarls.

Eleazar shows her his open palm.

"Hey, it's okay." His fingers shake. He pulls the pink collar out of his back pocket.

She takes a slow step toward him, then snaps. He pulls his

hand backward, barely escaping with his fingers.

Eleazar looks up at me with terror in his eyes. "I don't think this is Louisa."

The growling fake goldendoodle backs away and runs beneath the table. I bend over to look at her, but she has completely disappeared. She was never really here.

Eleazar looks like someone just ripped his heart out of his chest. "Etta, I'm scared," he admits. The subtitles beneath his face are small and squished together.

"Me too."

"What's happening?" he asks.

What's happening is that our story isn't over yet. Because the most important piece of it is still lost.

Louisa May Alcott is the writer who said we could find our castle in the sky, and she's the fluffiest goldendoodle in any world. We're going to save her, but we can't waste any time. The rest of the city is counting on us too.

And we've got one more train car to go. I shouldn't have second-guessed myself. My head was clearer in the storm than it is in here, surrounded by fake dogs and fake gifts. This isn't the real engine room. It's a fake made by Fide to throw us off.

My parents are still in trouble. And the real Louisa's still trapped. I'm not giving up on the promise I made to Eleazar. We *do* need to be rerouted—just not to Medellín. I use the keyboard beneath the map to type.

NEXT STOP: ENGINE ROOM

A red light flashes on one of the levers on the table.

The fake Keiko looks sternly at us. "My Master of the Maps and my engineer. I'm very disappointed in you. You're not thinking of going on, are you? Why would you leave such a perfect place?"

"Because perfection isn't real," I say. "It's almost always fake. *Ferfection*, they should call it."

"Don't say that," snaps Mariana. She stomps her foot. "You shouldn't talk to my mom that way. You don't know what she's been through to get back to me."

"Mariana," I say, lowering my voice. "Please come with us. You'll see—none of this is real. Your mom . . . isn't real."

"How can you say that?" Her eyes fill with hurt and tears. "I thought you were my friend."

She puts her arm around her mother. I need her to realize that we have to go home. Maybe that would snap her out of this. *But she always wanted to live here.* This was always her plan—fake mom or not.

The sight of them together makes me wish for my own mom. If I lost her, I know I'd take her back in any way I could.

"Okay," I say. "I'm sorry. You stay here. But we're going on."

I put my hand on the lever.

"I wouldn't do that," says Keiko. "You don't know what's on the other side. I bet your sickness won't be healed if you go on."

I don't like the way she sneers when she says *sickness*. It makes my fingers curl into fists.

I yank the lever down. The table moves aside to reveal a hidden door.

Eleazar and I enter the tenth train car.

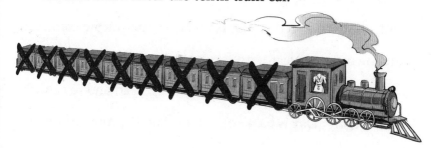

CHAPTER
22

AT FIRST the real engine room looks exactly like the fake one. Even the control table has all the same settings. The pointer's still stuck over VERY DANGEROUS, INDEED. There's no sign of Fide here either, but there are three big differences between the train cars. The first is that this engine has a big front window instead of a hidden door. We can see the storm outside, but the speed of the train slices the purple clouds in two, showing us a clear path forward.

The second difference is in my aching head and my sniffly nose. My Quiet Day is back to normal. And the final difference is the big rectangular cage in the middle of the room. It has thick golden bars. There's a goldendoodle inside.

Louisa?

She looks like the Louisa who stuck her head out of Eleazar's sweatshirt. Her eyes are dark and kind, and she's covered in fluffy curls. But I don't dare to hope. She'll probably try to bite me again.

Eleazar stands a few feet back from the cage. He's too afraid to move. A tear escapes my stinging eyes. This is terrible, not fair and not kind at all, to be teased with that fluffy face, only to have her snarl and turn against us.

The dog jumps up, presses her paws against the cage, and pokes her long pink tongue through the bars. She pants but doesn't snarl.

Eleazar takes a cautious step forward.

"Eleazar!" I say. "It could be a trap. Be—"

He reaches one hand through the bars. Louisa's tongue wraps around his finger. Eleazar kneels down in front of the cage. She jumps up to lick his face.

Suddenly I don't know where the boy starts and the dog

ends. It's as though there are no bars between them—Eleazar's hands are inside the cage, wrapped around Louisa's fluffy fur, and her snout sticks out of the cage, sniffing his hair excitedly.

I put my arms through the bars too—Louisa May Alcott's fur feels even softer than it did two days ago. She jumps up and down on her back two legs happily.

There's a door on the other side of the cage. Feeling confident that this Louisa is friendly, I pull the door. It opens.

Louisa May Alcott runs out of the cage and leaps into Eleazar's arms. He picks her up, but she's wiggling so much that she makes both of them topple over. Louisa lands on Eleazar's stomach, and he holds her there. Her nose nuzzles and licks every part of his face, and her tail wags as fast as windshield wipers on the bus.

I've never seen a dog so excited. I've never seen a boy so still.

She's real—I know for sure this time. There's no trace of a purple gleam in Eleazar's eyes.

It's really her. *We found her.*

This will be an illustration for my story and a memory to add to the word *friend*.

Eleazar gets up to scratch Louisa's head. Tears fall down his face; she licks them off. He looks at me, and his eyes say, *Thank you*, but it's not a regular thank-you. It's a thank you-*THANK YOU*.

This is joy, joy, *joy*, with stars dotting the *j*'s and answers for all the *y*'s.

I drop to my knees. Louisa May Alcott jumps up and puts both of her paws on my shoulders. She sniffs me, then licks my cheek. Her fur is soft, and it tickles my face.

Eleazar smiles up at me. I can almost make out another sentence in his eyes. *We got what we came for.*

I nod. "Now we just have to make sure there's a home to get back to."

My words show up under my chin again. "I guess the train is still giving some gifts," I say, gesturing at the subtitles. "And this one is actually nice."

"Do you think it translates for dogs?" Eleazar asks. "Louisa, speak!"

She tilts her head back, and the word, *Bark!* appears beneath her fuzzy chin.

✦✦

I look at the buildings outside the big window. We're back on our side of the city. Almost home. I breathe a sigh of relief, and then remember—getting closer to home only means we're bringing The Fear closer to the people we love.

But as we move, I see hundreds of lit windows in the buildings, shining like beacons through the smoke. Light to push away the darkness. Our city is fighting back.

A few yellow and blue sparks push some more of the purple clouds out of the real engine. Whatever those colors are, they're fighting back along with the people whose windows are lit, along with my parents and Eleazar and me.

But The Fear is still so big. I need to figure out how to make the other colors grow too.

I walk over to the control table. Next to the VERY DANGEROUS, INDEED pointer is a button that wasn't in the fake engine room. It's lit by a flashing green light, and it says AUTOPILOT.

Huh. That's weird. Without the Great Conductor, the train's been running on autopilot, taking whatever fuel it can get, even if that means it's running on mostly fear. I look again at the few sparks of yellow and blue. Maybe those little bits of good fuel are what helped us get through the train cars—what made the train give us clues and poems when we needed them.

I wonder what will happen if I turn the autopilot off. I don't dare push the button, but something beneath the console table catches my eye. I lean down and pull it out. It's a soft and shiny black jacket with white letters embroidered into the front. GC. The jacket isn't made of pure light, but there are sparkly reflective crystals embedded into the fabric. This belonged to the Great Conductor.

The door into the previous train car opens and shuts.

Mariana joins us in the engine room. She turns a key in a lock on the door and looks at us with a sad smile. The ringing in my ears returns, a sharp whistle warning me that she's not here because we're friends or because she decided to believe me about her mom. I don't want to be afraid of her, but there's something uncomfortable about her smile. Like she's faking it. The pointer on the meter moves again, searching for a setting even worse than VERY DANGEROUS, INDEED.

"What are you doing?" I demand.

"It's just for a little bit," she says. "I promise."

"You can't lock us in here," says Eleazar. Louisa May Alcott pants at his side.

Mariana avoids our eyes.

"What's going on in the other engine room that your mom doesn't want us to see?" I ask.

I'm not sure I want to know the answer. I try to steady my breathing.

Mariana's chest rises and falls as fast as my own. She's panicking too. The engine fills with more purple smoke.

"My mom said this is for your own safety. And it's just for a little bit while she reroutes the train."

"Where is she rerouting us?" I demand.

"She said she was looking forward to meeting Eleazar's grandmother."

"No!" cries Eleazar. "She'll bring The Fear with her."

Mariana looks away. She doesn't want to face us. *Does she know this is wrong?*

I think hard. There has to be a way to save the city while we're inside the real engine room. The poem we found in the painted forest said that we had to make a choice. Fear, or something else.

This can't all end with us trapped in here, watching the world outside the window collapse.

"Mariana, I think your mom was right about the Great Conductor." I lift the jacket I found. "Maybe we can still find out if the conductor exists . . . or take the train off autopilot and fix the engine ourselves or . . . I don't know exactly. That's why I need your help. Your mom's stories were true. Is there something else she told you that could help us?"

Mariana glares at me. "I don't want to hear any more about her stories! I shouldn't be talking to you at all. She only told me to watch you and make sure you didn't do anything suspicious."

Eleazar hugs Louisa May Alcott to his chest. I slump back against the wall. Even if I could get the key from Mariana or make a lunge for the autopilot button, I wouldn't know what to do next.

If Mariana doesn't have any more stories, maybe I can use mine. When I wrote about Fide, the train created her. Maybe if

I write the train a happy ending, it'll listen to that, too.

It's time for Invincible Girl to return. *My* Invincible Girl. Not the fake one.

I open my backpack and breathe a huge sigh of relief. The magic from the last train car wore off. The book turned back into my sketchbook. It's filthy from all our adventures, but it's mine. I flip through the paint-stained pages and find a mostly clean spot to write.

The memory of my fist colliding with the dragon's jaw fills my mind. I was almost like a hero then.

Maybe I can be one again. I wrote about Invincible Girl because I thought I wasn't strong enough to be a hero. But I can be strong without being unbreakable. Turns out, Invincible Girl wasn't all-powerful either. But she is brave. And so am I.

After all, I figured out that the last train car was a trap. I can get us out of this mess—as long as I believe-*believe* in my own story.

The one that'll fill these pages.

Someday. Suddenly, writing the perfect comic doesn't seem so important. Not with the train still broken, and my family still in danger.

I need to find a way to help them.

And I will. *I know I will.*

A dot of blue ink appears on a blank section of the sketch-book. It grows, stretches, and loops around, forming thick, curvy letters—the prettiest calligraphy I've ever seen.

> *Come, you dreamers, bring your pain.*
> *Hope will make us run again.*
> *For every wish, the steam will blow.*
> *Watch the city heal and grow.*

> *You are more than what you think.*
> *Fill the page with hopeful ink.*
> *And when all your wishes have come true,*
> *Go home, take heart, and start anew.*

It's another side to the poem we found among the trees. The other colors sparking in the engine. The force pushing back against The Fear.

Our other choice is hope.

CHAPTER 23

I WALK OVER to Eleazar and show him the new poem. Mariana stands in front of the door and crosses her arms, but she stretches her neck out to try to get a peek.

"What's that? What are you doing?" she demands.

I hold the poem away from her.

"Hope," repeats Eleazar. "That means there's another way."

"I think so," I say. Hope means possibilities.

There are swirls and sparks of blue and yellow flying around in the engine. *That's the fuel we need.* But the purple cloud swallows the colorful sparks like a magician swallows flames.

My eyes turn back to Mariana. I hesitate.

"Mariana, do you want to see this new poem? We can work together. We still need to fix the train."

"The train's not broken anymore," protests Mariana, but I see her swallow hard. "I have my mom."

Eleazar frowns. "If everything's okay, why did you lock us in?"

"To keep you safe—"

"Look out the window!" I say. "The Fear is still there."

"It doesn't matter. We're safe in here."

"But everyone else isn't," I say. "Is that a price you want to pay?"

She shrugs casually, but The Fear in her eyes betrays her. She doesn't want to let the city fall. *But who in the world would be willing to lose their mother twice?*

"Mariana, it's okay to be afraid. I am too." I hold up the new poem in my notebook. "But you said yourself that the train was broken. It's because we were giving it the wrong fuel. We need to be hopeful, not afraid. That's what Akio meant when he said we were bad cooks."

"We were using the wrong ingredients to fuel the train, right?" asks Eleazar. "The right ingredient is *hope*."

"I don't care," says Mariana. "If it's fear that's keeping Mom alive, then I don't care. I'm not afraid. I'm happy. For the first time since I left home."

"You are afraid," says Eleazar. "You're scared of losing her like I was scared of losing my home."

"And, Mariana," I say, "she *isn't* your mom."

She looks hurt, and angry. I don't want her to hate me. But I don't want to lose her to a lie either. I don't want to lose everything to fear.

"What are you trying to say?"

"You're still afraid! Look at the engine. It's *full* of fear. You're afraid of losing her, so you're settling for something less."

"You don't know anything!"

I blink away tears. A high-pitched ringing returns to my ears.

"I do," I say. "I can't stay here just because I'm afraid of what might happen when I go home. I don't want to live my life in fear, as a fake Etta. *Fetta.*"

Mariana turns away from me. "If I lose her, I'll have nothing."

A deep, painful THWACK throbs in my chest. *I'm not nothing.*

"That's not true. You'll have the train—the good one that

your real mom told you about. And you'll have us."

"You're just here to take the dog and leave. You don't really want to be my friends. And there was no Great Conductor. He wasn't waiting for me, like Mom said he would be. He must not care."

I feel the weight of the word *friend* again, heavier than ever.

"We could never have gotten through that storm without you taking our hands," I say. "We shouldn't have to go through any storms alone. I'll be your friend. I promise. You can trust us."

She shakes her head. The words beneath her chin wobble. "No one ever keeps their promises."

I hand her my sketchbook with the hope poem. I hand her all the other books in my backpack too.

Her eyes widen. "What are you doing?"

"Keep them. I know they're dirty, but there's still a few good spots. That part about the castle in *Little Women* is okay. And you can help me with my comic again."

"But . . . those . . . you love those."

"I know."

She reaches her hands forward, then snaps them back.

"They're a bribe. A trick!"

"No. They're a thank-you. And a promise. And you're wrong about the Great Conductor. He was here. I don't know what happened to him, but we'll help you figure it out."

I put the books down, and I give her the jacket I found. Eleazar pulls his copy of *Mujercitas* out of his bag. The one his grandmother gave him.

"We can all go to Colombia together, someday," Eleazar says. "I'll get another copy then. First, we go home."

"We go home," Mariana repeats. She blinks three times, and the flash of purple in her eyes disappears. She looks at Eleazar and me, waiting for one of us to say something else. We stay quiet. Louisa May Alcott walks up to her and rubs against her leg. Mariana hesitates, then taps the goldendoodle gently on her head.

She takes all the books, tucking the jacket gently under her arm.

A big swirl of blue and yellow sparks cuts through some of the purple in the engine. *Hope.* Mariana chose it too. But the fight isn't over yet. I wish I could take those sparks and seal them in the jar of courage inside my stomach. I'm going to need them soon.

"We have to find Fide," I say. "And Akio . . . and we have to say goodbye."

Mariana nods slowly and fumbles with the key. She's got too much stuff in her hands. She readjusts the jacket. Something falls out of the pocket.

Eleazar bends over and picks it up. I look over his shoulder. It's an old picture, but the man in it is definitely Akio. He's standing in front of the train next to Keiko, who's holding a baby. *And he's wearing the conductor's jacket.*

"Look at this!" I exclaim.

Mariana gasps. "It's him. It was really him all along."

"Akio is the Great Conductor. Why doesn't he remember?"

I think about his half-finished story in the train car with the painted trees. Something happened that made him forget.

Mariana rubs her thumb over the face of the woman holding the baby. Her eyes fill with tears. I look more closely at the woman. Her features are so familiar. They're shared by the girl standing in front of me, and her fake mom in the other engine room.

"Mariana," I say, trying to keep my voice steady. "Is that *you*?"

Mariana nods. Eleazar and I exchange a wide-eyed glance. "This must have been the last time my mom saw the train," Mariana says. "The last time she saw my grandpa, the Great Conductor. I didn't think there were any pictures of him."

"Akio's your grandfather?" Eleazar looks shocked.

"Did you know the Great Conductor was your grandpa?" I ask. "Why didn't you tell us?"

"I don't know. . . . The train wasn't what I thought it would be. Mom always said he would greet me as soon as the carpet rolled out. But he wasn't there. I was afraid that meant he didn't care about me. I didn't want you to know that."

"He must care about you," I say. "And he can take the train off autopilot! He can make sure it doesn't get any more fear and—"

"But he doesn't remember. He doesn't remember me or being the conductor or anything."

Mariana looks down at the picture, her face crumpled up with sadness.

"He's still your family, even if he doesn't remember. We

can't leave him in the storm," says Eleazar. Louisa May pants at his side.

"Family." Mariana repeats. She looks up suddenly, her face set with purpose. She clutches the picture, the jacket, and all the books to her chest, and forces the key into the lock.

We run back into the train car with the gifts-that-weren't-gifts.

Keiko turns on us.

"What's going on here? You're supposed to be watching them, not joining them."

"We found something. Look," says Mariana. Her voice is weak and pleading. She doesn't want to let her mom go yet. "It's Akio. Grandpa. He's trapped in the storm, and we need to save him."

"We have to take the train off autopilot so someone can drive it the right way," I say. "And the Great Conductor's the only one who can do that."

Mariana's mom glares. "*I* can drive it properly. We don't need him. Mariana, I asked you to do *one thing*."

Eleazar folds his arms. "Well, she needs to do one more thing. Right, Mariana?"

She nods. "I have to go get him. I'll be right back."

"You need to stay here," Keiko says firmly. When she speaks, the floor of the fake engine room vibrates, and all the screens flicker in and out. "Stay. Here."

The ringing in my ears is gone, but there's a voice in my head that taunts, *What if you don't save Akio? What if you get trapped in this fake engine?*

But I remember that that voice is just The Fear. I screw my eyes shut and turn my fear into a promise. *We will find him. We will make it out. We will, we will, we—*

Suddenly the door that leads back to the rest of the train slides open. Akio skates through and crashes right into the Fanksgiving table. Gravy and mashed potatoes fly across the room, splattering onto the TV screens and Louisa May Alcott's nose.

Mariana tackles him in a giant hug. His face wrinkles in alarm.

"What are you doing? Terrible cooks—"

His alarm doesn't seem to bother Mariana. She hands him the picture she found, and he takes it slowly. His face scrunches up like he's in pain, and he closes his eyes, but when he opens them again and stands up straight, he looks like a different Akio.

"Mariana?" His dark eyes are bursting with so much feeling and shock and hurt that my own eyes water and I almost wish I weren't watching them. It feels like stepping into something private.

"Grandpa? Do you remember me?"

"Mariana!" he cries. He picks her up, books and all, and they become a blur of skates and splattered cranberry sauce tears. Another big swirl of blue and yellow smoke cuts through some of the purple in the fake engine.

Akio sets her down.

"I thought you'd forgotten me," Mariana says.

"I did forget, for a long time. I'm so sorry. But I remember now. I remember everything." The pain flashes across his face again, and then he looks down and places a hand softly on Mariana's cheek. "You saved me. Did you come all this way for me?"

She nods.

"You are the bravest girl I've ever seen. How could I think that forgetting was the answer?"

"Because you really, really loved her. And you miss her. But she's here now. See?"

She gestures to the woman standing behind her, who watches them with eyes narrowed and fists clenched.

Akio skates in front of Mariana to protect her, but he can barely keep his balance. I don't know what it's like to see someone who looks like your dead daughter standing in front of you, but I bet he feels like his body's not his own.

"Who are you?" His face twists angrily.

"Grandpa, it's her. Maybe if I just show her this other poem—"

"She's not here," Akio says, staring directly into the fake Keiko's face. "She's gone."

"No, please. How do you know for sure? Maybe you forgot some part of the magic. You forgot so many other things."

Akio spins around and takes Mariana's face in his hands.

"You're right. I was so afraid of losing her that I gave up everything, every memory we ever shared. It wasn't worth it. Don't let the magic of the train tarnish your true memories of her."

"Please," Mariana pleads. "Please, I don't want to let her go."

"You can choose hope. For a new life. We all can. It doesn't mean we have to forget the old one, or try to change the past."

Mariana pushes past him and sets my books down so she

can reach for the woman. Her not-mother takes her hand but doesn't take her eyes off Akio.

Akio looks sadly at the woman. "It is okay to want to be near her. Take your time saying goodbye."

"No," Mariana protests. "I can't."

"Why don't you check and see if it's her," I say, as gently as I can. "Ask something only your real mom would know . . . the one who lived your mom's whole life."

Mariana knits her eyebrows together and doesn't move for a minute.

Finally she lifts her chin up and stares at her mother.

"Remember when you told me your favorite thing about the train? What was it?"

Mariana's mom smiles blankly.

She doesn't know.

"Please, don't you remember?"

"Who can remember such silly things?" she laughs. "We have the whole train to ourselves now. We can discover new favorites together."

Mariana takes a step back toward Akio.

"It wasn't silly. You said that your favorite part of the train was finding the right story for someone who needed it. I . . . I think you might be the wrong story."

The fake Keiko's light brown eyes flash purple. "So you want me to go?"

Mariana shakes her head. "I miss you so much. Don't go without saying goodbye. I didn't get to say goodbye before."

"Now you'll never have to."

"I do. Mama, I'm sorry. I'll find you in the storm again. Goodbye."

Keiko doesn't move.

"Please, just say it," says Mariana.

"Goodbye," she says, finally. And then she changes.

Her face morphs and her black hair turns blue. Her eyes turn purple.

She takes off her coat and turns it inside out. The other side is a white lab coat. She pulls huge goggles out of her pocket and pulls them down over her face.

She's Petra Fide.

CHAPTER
24

"YOU FOOLS." Petra Fide's words leave a slimy feeling in my chest. She pretended to be Mariana's mom. This Fide is a million times more evil than any villain I could write.

But she lives up to her name.

Mariana and Akio stare at the changed woman in horror. She didn't even have to use her lasers.

They're already petrified.

"You think you can stop me? It's too late. I've already won."

She can't have won. There's still hope, or I wouldn't have found that other poem.

Come, you dreamers, bring your pain. We have plenty of pain. We just need to dream up another solution.

"Give us another riddle," I say.

Eleazar steps forward. "And play by the rules."

"Fine," sneers Fide. "If you lose, you stay forever. As my fuel."

She wants us to fuel the train with fear for her. *Permanently.*

I think about the storm outside. The Fear will be permanent anyway, even if we don't agree.

"Okay," I say. Eleazar nods too. "We agree. Give us the riddle."

She pulls her blasters from some hidden place beneath the fake engine. She fires at the engine, and it explodes. Thick purple slime spills over the sides and slithers across the floor. Akio's skates slide through the slime, and he and Mariana fall. Eleazar and I rush to their side, and Louisa May Alcott tugs at the back of our shirts.

Fide slips by us and disappears through the door back into the storm.

Akio waves his arms at us. "Get out of here!"

"Are you okay? Can you turn the train off autopilot in the real engine room?" I ask.

"I'll take care of it, just go!"

Mariana hesitates, then hands him his conductor's jacket. He squeezes her hand tightly, and then Eleazar, Mariana, and I run. When we reach the door to the storm car, I stop, and make one more wish, and hope with all my heart that the broken train is listening.

We chase Fide back into the storm, with Louisa May Alcott at our heels. It feels like I got knocked over the head with the end of a blaster. The Fear swirls around us, but I have my own weapon now. I imagine hope as a shield protecting my lungs and putting the pieces of my jar of courage back together.

I reach back to hold on to Eleazar and Mariana. We've got to find Fide together.

BOOM!

A crashing sound busts through the River of Allergies. The ground beneath the storm shakes violently.

CREAK!

Something breaks the magic that makes the train cars look like whole worlds instead of steel boxes. I catch a glimpse of the roof above us before it flies right off the train car, disappearing into the sky above the city. Storm clouds twist their way out of the train car, clearing some of the air around us.

I see the roof floating in the sky. There are giant metal claws in it, and big wings flapping behind it. The dragon ripped it off. Its purple chest sends sparks raining down around us. The light-bulb eyes stare straight at me, blinking slowly on and off. I think I may be the next target, but at least it cleared out the storm. There are four walls to the train car now, with a door on either end.

And I can see Fide again. I could run forward and give her a big WHACK right to the face, like I did with the dragon. But I have a feeling my vertigo wouldn't like that. My body is tired. But deciding not to punch Fide in the face doesn't mean I have any less fight in me. It just means that I know who I am. So I back slowly into the corner, and I watch, and I wait. For the right opportunity.

Fide stands on the other side of the train car. She drops the blasters and puts two fingers in her mouth the way people do when they want to whistle really loudly.

The dragon releases the roof and flies down to circle right above our train car.

Fide speaks, and subtitles appear beneath her face. That was my final wish as we ran into this train car—and it worked. The train wants us to fix it. I can feel that now, as clear as the pull I felt when I first saw the fireworks. But The Fear is still messing things up, and the subtitles beneath Fide's face are blurry. I can only make out a few of the words. "Now . . . called . . . friend . . . have . . . fun!"

She lifts her arms and points at Mariana.

Her lips move again, but I can't make out any of what she says.

Mariana runs—but there's nowhere to go.

The dragon takes aim and blasts Mariana with The Fear.

Mariana freezes with her eyes open wide and falls back against the wall of the train car.

I feel a jolt of pain in my chest, like I've been blasted too.

Fide turns to Eleazar next.

"Here's . . . riddle . . . rocks . . . feed . . . but leaves . . . footprints . . . ?"

What? I have no idea what the riddle means. I couldn't see enough of the subtitles. I creep slowly along the wall, getting closer to Fide.

Eleazar's face fills with terror as he tries to back away from her. He doesn't know the answer to the riddle either.

Fide lifts her finger to point, but Louisa May Alcott snarls and leaps forward at Fide. She's one foot from biting Fide's finger off when the dragon hits her with The Fear.

Louisa doesn't freeze like Mariana. I remember what Akio said—The Fear doesn't affect animals. But still, the blast is strong enough to knock her over. She slides across the train car.

Fide laughs and points at Eleazar. She repeats her riddle.

I take a deep breath and focus, trying to fit the words I see together in a way that makes sense.

"What walks ... feet ... hands but leaves their footprints in ...?"

Something that walks, has feet and hands, and leaves its footprints? Maybe it walks on its feet and hands.

I stay as still as I can while Fide's lips curve upward and she speaks again, teasing Eleazar with all her extra chances.

Focus, Etta. Focus.

I get a little closer. I piece the jumbled and blurry letters into words, just like when I have to figure out what Dad is saying when he fingerspells.

"What walks without feet or hands but leaves their footprints in the sand?"

My mind runs through all the stories I've ever read, looking for clues.

"Invisible," I whisper, and then I say it louder. "An invisible person."

Fide looks around, confused. Her face looks twisted, tangled. This is almost fun.

I pick up one of the blasters from the ground and turn it on her.

But I'm too late.

The dragon crashes into the train car again. It curls its claws into the wall and pulls the whole train car onto its side, leaving us dangling above the edge of the elevated tracks, with nothing to stop us from falling out. My stomach flops. The Fear-covered city is below, ready to swallow us up.

No. I don't want to fall. Not after everything we've been through.

Louisa May Alcott scrambles to find her footing as the train veers from the tracks.

She slips over the edge.

"No!" cries Eleazar. He jumps after her.

"Eleazar!" I scream. *Be okay. Please be okay.*

Fide's smile starts a fire inside me. She doesn't get to win like this.

I drop the blaster.

"I created you," I tell her. "You're just a figment of my imagination, pieced together by magic. You can't defeat me, because you're part of me, and you always will be. And *I'm* the one telling my story."

Fide opens her mouth to taunt me again, but I'm sick of her riddles. I lift my finger and point at her.

The dragon obeys me, but the flames that come out of its mouth aren't purple. They're bright and colored like a rainbow. They surround Fide, and when the smoke clears, she's gone.

Her petrifying powers disappear along with her. Mariana gets up and races back toward the engine room to help Akio.

Eleazar's fingers grasp the edge of the train car. His other hand hugs Louisa to his body, holding her up.

I can't reach Louisa, so I try to grab Eleazar's hand, but it feels too slippery. Too dangerous. I'm not sure I'll be able to pull him up. The dragon hovers just outside the train car. I get an idea.

I may not be invincible, but I have hope to spare. Maybe even enough to turn a dragon into a friend. I reach my hand out, and the dragon flies toward me. Its metal nose touches the tip of my finger.

"You can make a choice too," I say. "I saw the hope in you."

Its light-bulb eyes blink twice. A small puff of green-and-yellow smoke escapes the dragon's nostrils. The dragon stretches its wings out wide, and some of the sparks inside its chest turn blue, yellow, and green instead of purple.

The dragon breathes fire. I try to hold my breath, ready for the wave of panic that'll fill my lungs, but the flames that escape between its giant teeth turn blue.

The blue flames feel cool and refreshing as they pass over me. They fill me with a feeling as pure and magical as that first

E in the sky. I feel something on my shoulders. *A cape*, bright blue and cloudlike. My feet rise a few inches off the ground. *I'm flying.*

I point at Eleazar, who's holding on to the train and Louisa. The dragon covers them with blue flames. Eleazar's eyes widen. He scrambles back into the train car and up the wall, his feet and hands sticking to every surface. A cape appears around Louisa May Alcott, too. The cape makes her stand upright like a human, and her back legs kick the air. She flies even higher than me.

The dragon nudges me with its nose. I give it a pat on the head. Mom is going to be concerned when she realizes I've become a dog person *and* a dragon person. The thought of Mom gives me another idea.

"Maybe you can help us," I say. "We could really use a friend to get rid of all these purple clouds."

The dragon's light-bulb eyes flicker softly, making contact with mine. It bows its head, and two small puffs of pink steam escape its glass nostrils, and float gently over my fingers.

Its wings flap beneath us, and it rises slowly, lifting the

train car back into place so we're right side up on the tracks. The train inches forward again, slowly but steadily.

The dragon takes off. I think it's headed for the city with a new mission. Its new flames overtake The Fear, and the sky begins to clear.

I feel strong and hopeful—*we saved the city*—but dizzy still.

"I'm going to rest awhile," I say. I crawl into the middle of the train car and place the side of my cheek against the floor. I stare at a spot on the wall until everything feels steady again. I don't know how long it takes.

When I finally sit up, Eleazar is sitting next to me. Louisa's head rests on my feet.

Eleazar's lips say, "Okay?"

I nod.

Eleazar points toward the front of the train with a question in his eyes.

"Okay," I say.

We're going back to the engine room. The real one.

But this time everything's different.

CHAPTER
25

I WRAP MY arms around Mariana as soon as I see her.

I feel the corner of my books—Mariana's holding them again—push into my stomach when we hug, like all that's between us are pages and words. If you're going to choose something to come between you and another person, stories are the best thing to choose.

I feel Eleazar's arms around us too, and Louisa May Alcott's tail wagging against my leg.

Better even than full-sentence eye contact: a paragraph hug.

We made a choice, it says. *Even though we don't know every-*

thing that's going to happen to us now, we look for hope. We made a
choice to be ourselves, but we don't have to be ourselves alone. We
can write a new story, one made for all of us.

That's the difference between the last two poems we found. In one you stay and get everything you want, but have to live in fear of losing it in order for the train to keep its power. Eventually fear will twist even your most magical dreams. It will trick you into thinking that you wished for something you don't actually need.

Like to be someone else.

Like to have a different story.

In the other poem you don't get everything. You have to go home. But you get a chance to fly, and you realize you can choose hope, even when there are shadows and scary unknowns. Hope fills in the blanks with bravery and friendship and ink as blue as a summer sky.

I walk up to the engine. The AUTOPILOT button is off. Akio's in charge now. He's making everything right again. The purple flames go out, one by one, until there are only a few left. A little bit of fear is normal. The pointer moves to THINGS ARE MOSTLY OKAY.

Maybe not all good yet, but enough to Go *home, take heart, and start anew.*

Akio skates around the TV screens.

"So you've been the Great Conductor all along," I say with a smile.

He sighs heavily. "Yes, but I've not been doing a very good job of it. All these children, with no one to help them. They've been alone for so long. The train's not supposed to pick up kids on autopilot. It should have stayed asleep."

Subtitles float around beneath Akio's chin. They're a pretty good substitute for a dead phone, but I can't wait to get home.

"What happened?" I ask.

"Mariana woke the train up when she found the map. She has a very strong will. And a connection to the train, through me. Keiko knew she'd be able to find me. And help me find myself. Unfortunately, I've been afraid for a very long time. So when the train woke . . . well, you know what happened. Things went wrong."

I smile. "It came for Eleazar and me. Even though it was on autopilot."

I look more closely at the TV screens.

"How does it work? How does it know which kids to bring on board?"

"When a child is looking for something but can't seem to find it—like courage or friends or knowledge—they show up on one of these screens. The train sends them an invitation with their name on it. Only people who are invited can see the train and their name in the fireworks."

"Kids who want their wishes to come true."

"Yes, but fulfilling wishes is the easy part. Figuring out your heart's true desire is where things get tricky. Sometimes when things are too easy, too magical, we realize that what we need isn't what we thought we wanted."

"Like how I didn't actually want someone to write my story for me."

Eleazar chimes in. "And how I should have just trusted my mom and talked to her about my grandma."

"You've done that for lots of kids?" I ask.

Akio nods. "We pick them up, keep them safe, show them about hope and fear, then drop them off. Sometimes there's more to be done—a few parents have come on board too—but that's usually how it works. The real treasure comes after you leave the train. It's out there, in the world. You'll find it."

I smile. "So Eleazar and I got a two-for-one invitation."

"Must be because you were so close to each other. Or because the train was malfunctioning."

I laugh.

"What's funny?"

"I thought Eleazar and I lived really far apart. Other sides of the neighborhood. I guess I hadn't seen so much of the city before. And when you add in Medellín, and everywhere else . . ."

"It's a big world. With lots of fear . . ." He waits for me to finish his thought.

"And lots of hope, too." I pause. "The story you couldn't remember back in the room with the painted forest. Do you remember it now?"

Akio looks thoughtful. "I do. I can't believe I lost so much. I tried to fill my heart with so many other things. Like cookies. Cookies! Can you believe it?"

"Yes," I say. "Cookies are really good. Can you tell me the rest of your story?"

He looks down at me, and I see he's not the same sleepy, silly Akio that I knew before. He's more serious now that he has all his memories of Something or Other. When he smiles at me, it's softer and sadder—the smile of someone who knows much more than I do.

"Would you like me to say it or paint it?"

Eleazar shudders. "No more paint, please."

"You could write it!" I say. "Fill your journal with something better than grievances."

"Good idea. Let's see, where to begin . . ."

He laughs and raises his eyes to look at me. They are clear and dark and full. Full to bursting, brimming with the weight of an ocean ten thousand leagues deep. A lifetime's worth of memories, heavy and happy and sad all at once. It makes sense now that he acted like a kid before, with roller skates and grasshoppers in his pockets. He didn't have his memories of anything else. He takes out a pen and his little book of grievances.

Once upon a time, there was a man who left behind silly made-up words and chocolate chip cookies and traded them in for a Regular Job as a train conductor. He missed being a child, and then he met a woman who missed it too. Her name was Shiori. They decided to have a child of their own.

The child's name was Keiko, and she was Joy Incarnate. She loved watching her father's trains speed by. The three of them had a wonderful life together. They stocked their home with cookies; they spoke in made-up words; they loved one another dearly.

Then Shiori passed, and they were terribly sad. Akio feared he would never be happy again. Keiko was sure they just needed something to bring them joy again. So they rebuilt an old train using Keiko's hope, and they set off on a wild adventure, bringing hope to children around the world. Magic gave them the freedom to do whatever they wanted, and the wisdom to choose to do the right thing. They grabbed all the hope they could. They gave it all away and made wishes come true.

Eventually Keiko grew taller than her father and started to fall in love with grown-up things—she read newspapers while wearing glasses, she left the train to go to work every morning.

Akio didn't see her for many, many years. She sent a letter every day; she even visited once with her own child, Mariana. And then she left to let the child be a regular child, but she promised she would bring the child to visit when she was older. And then one day, Akio learned Keiko could never come back. She was with Shiori. The memory of their love was too much, and he didn't like to be alone, so he let go. Of everything. He left the train with no conductor and forgot about everyone he loved. Without any hope for fuel, the train began to feed on Akio's fears. He let fear win. He didn't save the children who might have needed hope, but they saved him.

"But," I ask, "why does fear fuel the train? Why didn't you build it so that only hope can fuel it?"

"Because there's nothing wrong with fear. It's inside all of us. The problem is when we let ourselves get filled with so much fear that we give up and forget to hope. The train runs on all the colors—all of our emotions. It helps us process them. You shouldn't have to face your biggest fears, unfiltered, with no help. But without me the engine stopped processing fear and starting chugging it out into the world. It needs a tune-up."

"I said that! Eleazar, didn't I say the engine needs an oil change?"

Eleazar raises an eyebrow and smiles. "Etta, I don't think you know anything about engines."

I scrunch up my face at him, then turn back to Akio.

He sighs. "I never should have left the train on autopilot. It was too big a weight for this machine to carry, even as magical as it is."

"The magic started with Keiko. With Mariana's mom," I say.

"Now the engine has a bit of all its passengers inside. Everyone's wishes and dreams and fears. That's how it does the unimaginable. I told you it was alive, didn't I? Hmm, I can't remember."

I watch the engine and the small sparks of purple still mixing with the blue and yellow. There's purple in every rainbow. My heart feels full to bursting too. "It's okay," I say. "I understand. And now you're the conductor again. I guess I better let you get back to it."

Akio pulls a shiny gold hat out of some hidden pocket in

his jacket and places it on his head. He finds a smaller one too, and sets it on top of Mariana's curls.

"Shouldn't be too difficult now that I have a new apprentice," Akio says. "Would you like to see me conduct?"

"More than anything else." I smile.

"All right," he says, his words forming subtitles beneath his face. "It's been quite a while, but I'll show you."

He pulls a thin wand out of his pocket and skates through the door into the fake engine room.

CHAPTER
26

AKIO LEADS US into the train car that used to be the fake engine room. He must have used his own wish to remake it into a big orchestra hall. We're standing on a stage filled with a dozen folding chairs arranged in a half circle. There are instruments sitting on all of them—trumpets, trombones, and flutes. There's even a harp off to the side of the chairs. Akio skates to the front of the arrangement.

He begins to wave his conducting wand around in the air. The instruments rise from their chairs. Akio's crystal jacket shines in front of them. Mariana said the Great Conductor had instruments following him around and a uniform made out of pure light. Somehow, I think this is even better. I watch the strings on the harp rustle and the buttons on the saxophones and clarinets rise and fall. There must be a song playing, but I'm not sure what kind. The strings on the harp move gently.

It's all so different from anything I've ever seen that it almost stops feeling real. I watch the instruments the same way I read a book, with my mouth hanging open and my eyes scanning quickly from left to right. Eleazar looks as dazed as I feel. His fingers tap, tap, tap on the top of Louisa's fluffy head, keeping time with the rhythm. I tap my foot along with him and wonder if he's thinking about how cool an illustration the instruments will make too.

This isn't the sort of conducting I was hoping for, but all those instruments, floating on their own—they're beautiful. It's Quiet, but I can see the bows of the violins pressing softly against the strings. The trombone slides and sways at a slow, even pace. It feels like the eye of the storm, but a thousand times better. A sense of peace stretches my heart wide inside my chest, filling it with hope.

After a few minutes I clear my throat.

"Um, this isn't really the kind of conducting I was thinking of," I say, though I try to say it softly so I don't disturb the instruments.

Akio drops his wand and smiles. "I suppose not. Lovely, though, isn't it?"

I nod.

"Alas, you're out of time. The sun's about to set. If you want to see the other type of conducting, you'll have to come back another day."

He turns and winks at Mariana. Her face lights up. "Yes, please come back!"

The words floating beneath her face are bubbly and yellow.

"I'll bring you our new story." I look at Eleazar. "We are going to write a story, right?"

He grins. "The best one. I know how to run up walls now. I'll give Miles Morales a run for his money."

Mariana and I laugh.

"You were doing that before we ever got on the train," I say, reminding him of when he saved my sketchbook.

"Do you want it back—your sketchbook?" Mariana asks.

"Keep it," I say. "You can work on a story for us, too."

"How do we get home?" Eleazar asks.

The space in my heart filled with peace and hope gets even wider. *Home.* It's more than one place now. It's Chicago and Colombia and our Fanksgiving table. It's the train and Louisa May Alcott's fur and bright colors on a comic book page. It's wherever there's room for hope and blue clouds.

"Next stop: home," says Akio. He reaches out his right hand, and a handle immediately appears next to it.

We walk into a train car made entirely of glass. The sight of my feet standing right above the golden tracks makes my stomach do a double flip, but the vibrations are kind of nice. I look out into the city. Fluffy blue and green clouds blow out of the train's smokestack and over the buildings. The dragon flies in circles above us. In the distance the sun sets slowly. I missed Dad's curfew. My parents will never believe my excuse for why I'm late. I'm going to be in trouble for sure. But I don't care. I could use a break after all this adventure.

"Hmm, I think I'll drop you off in front of your house," Akio says. "I have a few more pickups to make down that way. And I don't want you small children walking alone."

"We saved the whole city," Eleazar says. "We're not that small."

Akio looks at me as though to say, *Pretty small.*

Then, without warning, the train lifts off the tracks and flies—*flies!*—up above the tracks.

Outside the glass I see my own, regular-sized house come into view.

The sparks in the engine swirl together, and I watch a rocket of color rise through the smokestack. The color explodes in sparkles, dancing across the sky like so many jewels.

"Did you just set off more fireworks? In *our* neighborhood?"

Akio shrugs and mutters something about an accident. His words appear in tiny smoke letters beneath his white-haired chin, almost too small to read.

The train lands in the middle of our street. Akio approaches the glass wall and takes a piece of chalk out of his pocket. He draws a large rectangle and then pushes it—a new door opens onto our street.

"Whoa," says Mariana. "I can't wait until I learn how to do that."

"You'll be an awesome conductor's apprentice," says Eleazar.

She stands up super straight and smiles. I turn to Akio.

"You're still worried you aren't brave enough," he says.

I nod. "Maybe a little."

"But you already did the brave thing, a long time ago. You decided to get on the train to help your friend and your family. And then you stayed, until the end, and that's more than courage. That's all you need."

More than courage. I like that. It feels like something Dad would fingerspell when he's telling me I'm like She-Hulk.

"Are *you* going to be okay?" I ask Akio.

He nods. "I've escaped Alcatraz."

Akio kneels down and scratches Louisa May Alcott under her chin.

"What about your grievances?" I ask him. "You said there were supposed to be no dogs allowed."

The sunlight coming in through the glass shines on Louisa May Alcott's fluffy fur.

"I will make this one exception."

CHAPTER
27

I STEP OFF the train with Eleazar. Another blue rocket shoots into the sky, and bursts into rainbow-colored sparks. The train flies off, but pieces of candy waft down from the exploded fireworks. Kids run out of their houses from both sides of our neighborhood and stick out their tongues to catch the sweetest rain.

Eleazar moves through the crowd. Louisa May Alcott walks right next to him without a leash.

The sun has come out just in time for it to go to sleep. It paints the sky with a deep orange the color of Mom's earrings, and I don't know what's prettier, the sunset or the fireworks. Together, they make something magical.

Mom and Dad must be feeling better now that the sun's back. My heart aches. I can't wait to see them.

We walk up to my steps.

My mom and dad are both in the kitchen, along with Eleazar's mom.

When Eleazar sees her, he puts his arms around her in another paragraph hug. I'm sure they have a lot to say.

Mom waves excitedly. She pulls me into a big hug, then pulls out her notebook and starts scribbling away. *Give me your phone.*

"What?" I ask.

You didn't respond to most of my texts. You're on punishment.

"It died!" I protest, even though I knew this was coming. "Not my fault."

Then I guess we'll have to get you a battery pack. And a better GPS tracker. For when you're off punishment.

"How long?" I ask.

As long as I say.

Mom holds out her hand expectantly, and I hand over the phone. She plugs it into a charger in the kitchen. Even with The Fear gone, Mom is still Mom. And I love her—*love her*.

She hands me her own phone. I read her lips. "For translating."

"The scientists still can't explain that huge storm today. They've been trying to work it out," Dad says. "But Eleazar's mom was worried, and I admit, I've never been so scared."

The Ms. Suzy app and the magical subtitles are gone, but that's okay. I scoot closer to Dad.

"There was so much chaos everywhere, and we couldn't even get in touch with you," he says. "The storm messed up your phone's location and everything."

Dad shudders at the memory of it. I don't like the thought of him filled with The Fear, wondering where I was. But he's not filled with The Fear now. *And I had something to do with that.*

"But then"—Eleazar's mom laughs—"when I got here, we

started talking, and it helped us feel like everything would be okay."

Talking. Yeah. I'm sure that's what helped make them feel okay. Definitely not the fact that we survived dragon fire and saved the whole city from falling to The Fear.

Mom is staring suspiciously at Louisa May Alcott, who decided to sit right on top of Mom's feet. "I'm glad you found her, but look at those paws. They're tracking dirt on my carpet. Yuck."

I read the words on her phone screen and try to make my own eyes look like puppy eyes. "Mom, come on," I say. "She's so cute. Let her stay."

"You're allergic!"

Eleazar jumps in. "She's a goldendoodle. They're for people with allergies."

Dad looks thoughtful. "Maybe we should get one. I heard you don't even have to vacuum up after them much."

He winks.

I scratch Louisa's soft ears. "See, Mom? I'm not allergic."

"Where'd you find her?" asks Dad.

"Uh, the train . . ." I look back outside the window, but the train's probably far away by now. There are still kids eating candy in the street.

"The train station? So she came back, huh? What a good girl," says Dad, scratching Louisa's ears. He follows my gaze out the window. "What's going on out there? Some kind of block party?" He fingerspells *block party* as he speaks.

I grin.

"You two hungry?" asks Mom.

Dad starts pulling all the leftover containers out of the fridge. He sets the table while Mom heats stuff up and puts a lot of extra salt out for Eleazar and his mom, already apologizing for the under-seasoned food.

Mom brings out some folding chairs from the closet.

Everyone squeezes in around our little kitchen table.

Eleazar's mom gets a video call from his grandma, who can't figure out how to turn the video camera on her phone the right way.

Still, she's there. And Eleazar is beaming.

When they're saying goodbye, Eleazar's grandma says, "See you in two months!"

His mom frowns, then laughs nervously. "Don't be silly. We won't see you in two months."

I remember what they said to each other when we were watching from the train.

Eleazar pushes his hair out of his face and looks at me with his eyebrows raised.

"It's my birthday in two months. Am I getting a surprise or what?"

He smiles.

We both sign at the same time. "Awesome."

There are times in life when everything changes. Maybe the change is something cool, like new friends or arepas, but other times it's scary. All you can do is accept it, and be brave enough to keep going until you face the next change, and the next one and the next one, until you're older than Akio. You don't have to be the bravest or the most fearless. You just have to be brave enough to choose hope. I think that's what Akio meant when he said staying until the end is *more than courage.*

Somehow we convince Mom to paint a portrait of Louisa. She goes upstairs to get started right away.

"When the muse hits, it hits," she signs to me. She even reaches down to pet Louisa before she leaves.

I grab a pen and a few sheets of clean paper from a drawer— no spilled ink or creepy trees here—and sit in front of our coffee table next to Eleazar. Two days ago all I wanted was a perfect story I could finally show someone without getting embarrassed. But now I want something different: to *share* my story, not just show it off. To share it with a friend.

I write, *Time to write our story.*

Eleazar takes the pen. He starts to sketch a picture of something. . . .

A school bus.

I write across the top, *Invincible Girl Rules the World, Part Two.*

No, Invincible Girl doesn't need another story. We need something better. Something even stronger. I try again.

ACKNOWLEDGMENTS

Thank you to my agent, Danielle Burby. I'm so grateful to have you as an advocate and champion for my work. Thank you for never letting me disappear when it feels like disappearing would be easier. To my wonderful editor, Alyson Heller, thank you for sticking with me and Etta through the strangest and hardest of times. Your insights and support mean the world. Thank you to art director Laura Lyn DiSiena, for the amazing cover and comic design, and illustrator Gretel Lusky, who brought Etta and Eleazar to life in such a beautiful way.

To my Chicago writing friends: Rosaria Munda, Lizzie Cooke, Rena Barron, Mia Manansala, and Layne Fargo. Thank you for all the writing retreats and coffees and conversations. I feel so lucky to have found our community.

Thank you to the loveliest humans: my critique partners, Jennifer L. Brown, Bronwyn Clark, and Remy Lai. From meeting on the internet to New Orleans and New York—I'm so glad you're all in my life! Thank you for reading my long-winded emails and cheering on Etta for all these years.

My Pitch Wars mentors and friends, Jessica Vitalis and Julie Artz. Thank you for seeing something in my work. You believed in me from the very start, and I wouldn't be here without you. Thank you for reading *Etta* eight thousand times.

Thank you to my best boy, Johnny Dogs. I realize that you are a dog and probably can't read this, but thank you for snuggling by my side and keeping my toes warm on long writing days. I'd fight a comic book villain to get you back any day.

Thank you to my family, the Eschflixes and the Pizzingtons, for being my best source of support and encouragement. Pyne fam, thank you for listening to me talk about publishing and for being excited about my work. Malachi, Karis, and JD, thanks for being the coolest and most creative kids around. Looking forward to your critiques. Mom and Dad, thank you for loving me unconditionally and having the audacity to believe I could be anything I wanted. My big brother, Rob, I started writing because of you. You will always be the person I dress up as on hero day. I can't wait to see what's in store for the Blinklings!

My husband, Danny, thank you for being so proud of me that it makes me feel I ought to be proud of myself too. You're my best friend, and if I could fill a magical train car with gummy bears for you, I would. I love you.

And finally, above all, thanks to God, who wraps me in clouds of peace when fear threatens to take hold, whose wisdom guides me and reminds me that tribulation brings about perseverance; and proven perseverance, character; and proven character, hope; and hope does not disappoint.

ABOUT THE AUTHOR

Reese Eschmann holds a master's degree in social work from the University of Illinois at Chicago and worked in schools for six years. When she's not writing or taking naps, Reese enjoys rock climbing, baking, and making movies with her family. She lives outside Chicago with her husband and their hound dog. *Etta Invincible* is her debut novel. Find her on Instagram and Twitter @reesespieces21_ or at ReeseEschmann.com.